OUTAGE 2: THE AWAKENING

By T.W. Piperbrook

ABOUT **OUTAGE 2:**
THE AWAKENING

Tom Sotheby has escaped the forest, but he is far from safe. His wife has been butchered. The town he once knew is a barren white wasteland.

And the beasts won't rest until he's dead.

His only hope is to get to town, to safety he isn't sure exists...

Want to know when the next release is coming out?Sign up for NEW RELEASE ALERTS at:http://eepurl.com/qy_SH

Prologue

Tom Sotheby pounded the wheel of the SUV, his eyes alternating between the forest and the road. He revved the accelerator, listening to the tires scream, but the vehicle remained hopelessly stuck in the snow. He wasn't safe. Not yet.

"Come on, you piece of shit!"

Growls and commotion spit from the trees, reminding him of the grisly scene he'd escaped. He let his foot off the gas pedal, then stomped it again. The wheels spun. Even if he survived the night, he had no idea what would become of him. His wife Lorena was dead. Gutted like a piece of meat. And he was next.

I can't believe Lorena's gone...

And so was Abby.

He felt a pang of sorrow for the girl he'd rescued. She'd been one of them. She'd been bitten, and she'd turned. In the throes of her transformation, she'd thrown herself into the fray and traded her life for Tom's.

He couldn't let that be in vain.

He dried his tears and glanced at the passenger's seat, eyeing the rifle he'd managed to salvage. The gun was empty. Even if it were loaded, it'd be useless against the creatures in the forest. He'd already spent his ammunition and failed. He had no extra rounds. In the frenzy of his escape, there'd been no chance to grab Abby's gun.

What the hell *were* these things?

He'd never seen anything like them. From what he could tell, they used to be human, but they'd become something else—beasts with claws and fur, elongated noses, and pointed teeth. Animals birthed for hunting.

He toggled between reverse and drive. The SUV lurched back and forth. The road was bathed in snow—eight inches, if he had to guess. It'd been difficult to drive a half hour ago, and it would be even harder now. He stared through the cracked windshield, watching snow spit from the sky. The wipers scraped back and forth over fractured glass.

Squeak... squeak...

"Come on!"

The four-wheel-drive was engaged. Even with the extra power, the SUV wouldn't move. Tom peered through the driver's side window, certain the beasts were almost upon him. The noise in the forest had ceased. They must've taken care of Abby.

They'd be coming for him next.

Tom revved the gas again. If he couldn't get the SUV moving, he'd head out on foot. There was little hope he'd outrun the beasts, but he'd damn well try. Sweat trickled from his brow and adhered to his face. He could see his breath in front of him. Even with the heat on, the vehicle was freezing—cold air poured through the cracks in the windshield, and it fought against the warmth.

The tires spun.

Tom gritted his teeth and grabbed for the empty rifle. He reached for the door handle, ready to flee. He stopped when he saw what was waiting for him.

A pack of shadows had emerged from the forest. He saw a glimmer of red eyes, the glint of claws and teeth. The beasts raced toward him. He drew back and mashed the door lock button, then shifted into drive.

He dropped the rifle in his lap and slammed the gas pedal.

Move, you son of a bitch!

The vehicle climbed and stopped, climbed and stopped. The beasts were three hundred feet away, spewing from the forest like ants from a dirt mound. He watched as they loped faster, gaining ground. Tom pushed the pedal to the floor.

"Goddammit! If this thing would just—"

The vehicle lurched. Miraculously, the tires grabbed the snow and stuck, and suddenly the SUV was rolling down the snow-blanketed street. Tom's heart pumped faster with each rotation of the tires.

Holy shit...

The things veered from the woods to the road. Closing in.

Tom couldn't tell how many there were. At the moment, they were nothing more than a myriad of shadows, a legion of creatures that seemed like they'd come from hell to take him.

Maybe he *was* in hell. He could think of no better explanation.

The world had transformed from something he knew to something he didn't. Gone were the familiar, paved streets that he'd known; all that was left was this barren white tundra—the perfect killing ground for the beasts.

The SUV gained momentum, but not fast enough. Tom heard a scraping sound along the driver's door and looked over to find a furred hand at the window. He cried out and let go of the steering wheel, instinctively protecting his face. The thing clawed at the pane, raking its nails along the slippery glass.

"Get away from me!" he shouted.

He snatched the empty rifle from his lap. He knew it wouldn't do him any good, but his instincts had taken over, and they screamed at him to do *something*. He held the weapon against the window, as if the mere sight of it would dissuade the beast, but the thing continued to scratch the glass. Its eyes were red and inhuman.

The vehicle picked up momentum, and Tom fought to stay on the road. The thing growled at him through the window. After a few more moments, the beast slipped from the car. The rest of the creatures lagged behind. He stared at them in the rearview mirror—dark demons with red eyes. Watching. Waiting.

Their motives were simple: they wouldn't rest until they got to him.

And when they did, they'd rip him apart.

PART ONE – THE COLLAPSE

Chapter One

Two hours earlier...

"What's going on, honey?" Lorena stood at the porch door, peering into the garage at Tom. She folded her arms across her pajamas and rubbed her eyes.

"I'm starting the generator," Tom said. "The power's out."

He shined the flashlight on the gas can in front of him.

"It's freezing in here. Did you see all the snow?" Lorena asked.

"Unbelievable. And in October, to boot."

"You're not late for work, are you?" Lorena whispered in the semi-darkness.

Tom rechecked the time on his cell phone. It was one in the morning—much too early to think about work. For the past few months, he'd worked the weekend shift as an elementary school janitor, trying to earn extra money. He normally didn't leave until four o' clock. Weekdays were spent at the manufacturing plant.

"It's still early. I'll catch a few more hours of sleep before I head in. Maybe I'll get dressed before I lay down, so I won't wake you up."

"The roads are covered in snow, Tom. Do you think it's safe?" Lorena asked.

She shifted in the doorway, her voice wavering. Tom glanced over at the SUV. If there was one thing he knew, it was that there was no way to guarantee safety in weather like this. He swallowed his concern.

"I'll take the Highlander. I'll be fine."

Lorena didn't argue. He could tell she was still nervous. Tom double-checked the generator's gas tank, verifying it was full, then set down the gas can.

"I'm going to open the garage and vent the fumes, honey. It'll get cold fast. Why don't you head inside? I'll meet you in a minute," he said.

Lorena reluctantly agreed, shuffling back into the house and closing the door. Tom shone the flashlight on the generator, replaced the gas cap, and walked over to the wide, single-bay garage door. He reached for the handle. The metal was cold against his fingertips, reminding him of how cold *he* was. Tom was still in his pajamas, and the chill of the garage was arresting.

He pulled up the garage door.

Opening the garage was like exposing another world. Tom stood at the threshold, peering out at the stark white neighborhood. The houses were covered in soft, rounded edges; the roofs were blanketed in snow. White pellets flung their way past Tom and into the garage, as if they, too, were trying to escape the nasty weather. The houses in the neighborhood were silent and still. No one was awake.

At least, not that Tom could tell.

"They're probably better off," he muttered.

He looked back at the generator. He felt guilty about starting it, but his house was set back from the road. Hopefully he wouldn't disturb anyone. He didn't want to subject Lorena to the cold.

She'd been through enough over the last few years.

Shrugging off his reservations, he walked back into the garage and wheeled the generator so the exhaust was facing outside. Then he pulled the cord. The engine roared to life. He peered outside guiltily, but saw no evidence that he'd woken anyone.

He padded back through the garage and to the kitchen door, shaking off his boots. Then he opened the door to the mudroom and reentered the house. Lorena was waiting in the kitchen. She was holding a flashlight of her own.

"Why don't you head back to bed? I'll meet you in a minute. I have to switch on the power in the basement."

"It's okay. I'll wait here for you." She smiled. "You're not going to blow snow tonight, are you?"

"No, I'll wait until tomorrow after my shift."

Tom played the beam of his flashlight upward a little, exposing her face. Lorena's eyes were soft and kind. At forty-five, she looked better than when they'd married. Despite that, Tom still saw the sadness that lurked below her expression. The loss of their son Jeremy still hung between them, even when they didn't speak about it.

Tom leaned over and kissed her, promising he'd be right back.

"Don't go wandering around in the dark," he warned.

"I won't," she swore.

He headed for the basement, opened the door, and made his way down. As he descended the stairs, he heard the dull drone of the generator through the walls. He wondered how widespread the outage was. Was the whole street out of power?

Was the whole town?

There was a chance Tom would arrive at the elementary school in a few hours and be without power. If that were the case, he wouldn't be able to do much. But he'd make the attempt. Tom always prided himself on being reliable, and he didn't want to miss his shift. Besides, he needed the money. They were fixing up the house. Once it was renovated, they'd sell it.

That was the promise he'd made Lorena.

He played the flashlight over the basement, revealing the oil tank, the hot water heater, and the circuit breaker. Next to the circuit breaker was a single lever. He'd installed the generator so that it was easy to use. When the lever was pulled, the house switched to the hookup in the garage. He wanted to ensure Lorena was always provided for, in case something happened. It was a morbid thought, but it was better to be prepared. The future could be callous and unpredictable.

Jeremy's death had proved that.

Jeremy had died during a winter storm like this one. Three years ago, he'd been driving home from a friend's house when he'd skidded off the road and flipped over a guardrail. Tom would never forget the moment the police had come to the door. He could still recall the officer's somber face. Since then, every snowstorm was a reminder of Jeremy's passing—both for him and Lorena.

Tom bit back his emotion and walked the remaining steps toward the circuit breaker. He shined the flashlight and pulled the lever. From upstairs, he heard the creak of a floorboard— probably Lorena waiting for him. Her uneasiness transcended the space between them. He tucked the flashlight under his arm and reached for the light switch.

A *thud* emanated from the backyard.

What the hell?

Tom paused. He swiveled toward the rear of the house and listened. All was still. He waited a second, then reached for the light switch. The thud came again. He grabbed the flashlight and shined it at one of the rear windows, looking for the source of the disturbance. Snowflakes drifted past the small pane. The window was at ground level; the lower half was obscured with white powder. He could barely see outside.

Tom crept across the basement toward the window, leaving the light off.

"Lorena?" he hissed in the direction of the stairwell.

Nobody answered. The noise came again. It was definitely from somewhere out back. Tom kept his eyes glued to the small window, afraid to look away, afraid he might miss whatever it was. Was it a burglar? Was someone trying to break in?

He thought of his gun—upstairs in the bedroom, tucked in the closet.

It was two floors away, much too far away to get to it quickly. But he wouldn't panic. Not yet. He'd see what the sound was before alarming Lorena. It was probably something normal, something explainable.

He didn't want to frighten his wife unnecessarily.

He stole past his tool bench until he'd reached the basement window, then stood on his tiptoes and peered over the windowsill, aiming his flashlight. When he looked above the snowdrift, he was surprised to find the yard was illuminated, even in the middle of the night. The moon crept stealthily from behind the clouds.

He never recalled seeing the moon during a storm.

That's strange, he thought.

The backyard was a white replica of the one he knew. Snow decorated the trees, the yard, and the deck. Nothing was out of order. No animals.

No intruders. He scoured the landscape. After a minute, he located the cause of the disturbance. Two medium-sized branches had fallen in the yard. Snow and leaves clung to the sides, making impressions in the white-covered ground. The limbs must've broken off with the weight of the snow.

It was strange, but explainable.

Relieved, Tom returned to the light switch and flipped it. The room brightened. At the same time, the furnace kicked on with a rumble, filling the basement with sound. Lorena's footsteps arose from upstairs.

It was as if restoring the power had returned everything else to normal.

Tom sighed with relief and flicked off his flashlight. Before heading to the stairs, he took one last glance out the window, watching quiet snow flit past the pane.

He sighed and headed back upstairs.

Lorena was waiting for him by the kitchen window. The kitchen light was on. She stared out into the backyard, her eyes locked on the landscape. She spun as he entered. She must've seen the concern on Tom's face. She frowned.

"Everything okay with the power?" she asked.

"Yeah. Everything's fine. I heard some tree branches falling in the backyard, that's all. They startled me."

Lorena pointed out the window. "I know—I saw them. Another one just fell in the woods."

Tom nodded. "It's because of the early snow. It must be weighing them down. I don't recall ever having a storm like this in October. It's very strange."

Lorena lowered her gaze.

"You all right, Lorena?" he asked.

She nodded, tears glistening in her eyes. He knew what she was thinking about, because he was thinking the same thing.

"I wish you didn't have to work," she whispered. "The roads are only going to get worse."

Tom took his wife's hand. "Don't worry, I'll be careful. I'll be home before you know it. I need this job, honey. Once we get the place updated, once we get the contractors in here..."

They'd talked about moving for over a year. Their plan was to go down south. After Jeremy had died, the house had become a mausoleum, a place to hang their coats and eat their meals. Nothing more.

"Let's head back upstairs and get some sleep," Tom suggested.

He turned on the hall light and snapped off the light in the kitchen, then led his wife to the staircase. They climbed the stairs and reached the hall, making their way into the master bedroom.

The alarm blinked twelve o'clock. Tom set the time and put on his work clothes. Then he placed his boots near the bed. He climbed beneath the sheets, where Lorena was waiting. She reached over and took his hand, giving it a squeeze. He doubted she'd be able to sleep. He wouldn't, either.

He'd have to get up for his shift soon, anyway.

The generator pulsed from the garage. Tom wondered how his neighbors were making out. One or two had generators, but not all of them did. There was a possibility one of them would come to the house in the morning.

If so, that was fine with him.

Tom closed his eyes and let his mind drift. Every so often, a branch cracked and fell outside, but he ignored it. A car started outside. Then another. He assumed his neighbors were leaving to get somewhere warm. He ignored that, too. He needed to get rest; otherwise he'd be exhausted for his shift.

He contemplated what he'd do after work. When he got home, he and Lorena would spend the day together. They'd make the best of the situation. They'd make hot chocolate and watch television, and he'd blow snow. Someday, someday *soon*, they'd leave the house behind and move. They needed a fresh start.

A scream wrenched him from his thoughts.

Tom bolted upright in bed and flung the sheets aside, heart knocking.

"What was that?" he hissed.

Lorena stirred beside him. She reached out and touched his arm, as if she were afraid he'd vanished. Tom swung his legs off the bed, the floor cold against his socks. He climbed from bed and started for the window, his pulse climbing. He parted the shade and looked outside.

What he saw made his body tremble.

In the middle of the road, something he couldn't identify — a furred animal, a *creature* — was tearing into one of his neighbors. Tom's blood froze. Whatever the thing was, it was larger than a man.

"Oh, my God..." he whispered.

"What is it?" Lorena breathed from across the room.

"Lorena, get the gun!"

Chapter Two

Tom stared out the bedroom window while Lorena ran to the closet. His legs felt rooted in place. The man in the street was Desmond Smith, his neighbor. Desmond was being mangled. His stomach was torn open and he was screaming. The beast had its back turned, but Tom saw bits and pieces of its visage — hands that resembled claws, a gaping maw; a snout larger than any animal he'd ever seen.

"Lorena! Hurry!"

Tom lunged for his boots. He frantically put them on. Behind him, Lorena threw the closet door open, rifling through objects to get to the gun. Tom let go of the shade and ran for his wife. He saw her shadowed form making its way back to him. She had the gun. Tom reached out and took it, staving off the panic that filled his stomach. He'd never used it before. *Not for something like this.*

Tom clicked off the safety and raced back to the window. Desmond had stopped screaming. His carcass lay motionless in the snow, his remains strewn across the snow-covered street. The creature loped in the other direction, making its way toward Desmond's house. Tom saw flashes of movement through the open doorway. Another creature—identical to the first, only larger—was already inside. A scream erupted from the top floor. Probably Tori Smith, Desmond's wife. Further down the street, another creature burst through a window, spraying glass into the snow.

The things were everywhere.

Lorena came up beside him and clasped her hand over her mouth, stifling a scream. Tom spun her away from the window just as a series of bangs erupted from downstairs. He swallowed as he recalled the open garage. It was only a matter of time until one of the things burst into the mudroom, then the kitchen. He didn't even have any idea what *they* were, what might be happening, but he knew he had to react. If he didn't, he and Lorena would die.

"Come on!"

He grabbed his cell phone off the nightstand and raced to the bedroom door, glancing frantically around the room. He considered pushing the bureau in front of the door, but the screams outside told him it wouldn't make a difference. The house felt like a cage with four walls, a trap rather than a place of safety.

The basement...

If they could get down there, maybe they could lock themselves in the furnace room. Call the police. The door was sturdy. Maybe he'd push the shelves in front of it.

"Downstairs!" he hissed.

Tom aimed his gun as they crossed the bedroom threshold. He peered down the stairs. The house suddenly felt dark and foreboding, *menacing*. He was suddenly certain one of the things was already inside, waiting to pounce. He kept the lights off. Anything he did might draw their attention.

They crept down the stairs one at a time, staring at the front door. Lorena gripped his arm as if she were falling off a ledge, her nails digging into his skin. The glass windows beside the door were frosted with ice. With each step, Tom saw a blurred piece of the street—houses and yards, snow whipping past. When they were halfway down, Tom caught sight of Desmond's body. The man was flat on his back, his carcass covered in gore. His wife, Tori, was sprawled next to him. She was already dead.

One of the creatures must've dragged her outside.

Tom shuddered and took another step, peering right and left up the street. The neighborhood was a replica of similar scenes. Opened doors, shredded bodies. *They're dead. All of them.*

Even without seeing his neighbors, he knew, the same way he'd known Jeremy was dead when the police knocked on his door. And he knew they'd be next if they didn't hurry.

"Come on!" he hissed, urging his wife downstairs.

They'd just reached the landing when something slammed against the front door. Tom and Lorena froze. A fur-covered hand raked the glass. Tom glanced back at the staircase, contemplating running back up to the bedroom. The porch creaked with the weight of the creature. He could sense the thing on the other side of the door, just as he was certain it sensed *him*.

He aimed his gun as a red eye pressed against the glass.

"Stay still," he hissed to Lorena through clenched teeth.

Lorena stiffened next to him; Tom's breath caught in his throat. The creature's breath fogged up the window. Tom saw the glint of teeth, a black, snarled face. After a few seconds, the beast vanished.

Where was it?

Tom and Lorena took another step. A roar escaped from the other side of the door—a terrifying, primal sound unlike anything Tom had ever heard.

And then the door buckled.

"Go!" he shouted.

They raced from the foyer into the dining room, skirting chairs, passing the dining room table. Tom's boots slipped and slid on the hardwood, as if the house itself was conspiring to kill them. Adrenaline coursed through his body, propelling him faster. He moved by muscle memory alone, darting through the kitchen without the assistance of the lighting, each step enveloping him further in darkness.

Behind him, the front door caved.

Lorena lost her grasp on his arm, but stayed right beside him as they reached the basement door.

He'd just grabbed hold of the door handle when a window shattered in the den. Lorena screamed. Feet pounded from the rear of the house, crunching over glass. *They're inside! The things are inside!* Tom flung open the basement door and stared into the darkness, ready to forge down into it. But a voice in his head stopped him.

Don't go down there.

The thought hit him with such force that he reeled backward. They couldn't go down to the basement. If they did, they'd never leave.

"Come on!"

At the last second, Tom changed direction, pulling Lorena with him. Her panicked gasps echoed through the kitchen. He groped the kitchen counter in search of the keys, finding them right next to the microwave where he'd left them. He snagged them as he ran to the mudroom door, clawing at the lock. He'd opened the damned door a million times before, but between the adrenaline and the terror, his fingers felt numb and useless. *Come on!*

"Hurry, Tom!"

Something bounded through the kitchen behind them. Tom unlocked the door and flung it open, barreling through it and into the mudroom, Lorena almost toppling him over. Tom spun, trying to pull the door closed. But the creature was already at the threshold, pawing the air. Tom raised the rifle and fired.

The blast echoed through the doorway.

The gun shook in his hands; the creature toppled sideways. It slammed against the kitchen counter, scattering several dishes onto the floor. Tom could barely make out its features in the darkness.

But it wasn't dead. It kept coming.

"Go!" Tom screamed.

They bolted through the garage door and into the garage, almost falling down the steps. They were immediately hit with a blast of white. Between the light of the sky and the falling snow, the garage was bathed in an ethereal glow. The generator spat loudly from across the bay. There was just enough room to get the SUV out around it.

"Get in the car!" Tom shouted.

He ran to the driver's door of the SUV and squeezed the unlock button on his keychain. He ripped the door open and leapt inside. As he inserted the key in the ignition, he prayed the vehicle would start. It did.

He searched for Lorena, who was already at the passenger's door, opening it and jumping inside. His head snapped to the garage. The creature was in the bay, hurtling toward them. Tom reversed. He gunned the accelerator, flinging his arm over the seat, narrowly avoiding the front wall of the garage and the generator, his only intention to get *out* and away from the madness.

Lorena screamed. Her shriek sounded far away, as if she were across a canyon rather than sitting in the seat next to him.

Something crashed into the hood of the vehicle, but Tom kept going, steering backward until he reached the road. He heard a thud as something fell off the vehicle. He switched into drive and hit the gas. In the rearview, several more creatures emerged from the houses, carrying bodies covered in gore. The neighborhood Tom had known was gone, replaced by a sickening mixture of red and white.

Tom gritted his teeth. He kept driving.

He didn't stop, not even when he hit the main road.

Chapter Three

Holy shit, holy shit...

Tom struggled to control his breathing. He and Lorena drove through the snow-ridden streets, searching for signs of life. The houses around them were dark, the driveways empty. It looked like most of the occupants had left before the storm got bad.

"What's going on?" Lorena whimpered.

"I don't know, honey. I don't know."

Tom barely felt coherent. His mind spat images of what he'd seen. Without the creatures in front of him, he questioned his vision and his sanity. Was he living some nightmare, some twisted hallucination? For a few moments, he entertained the possibility that he was still in bed, that he'd imagined the bloody scene.

Was he having a night terror? God knows he'd had plenty of them after Jeremy died. But Lorena was here next to him, and she'd seen it, too.

If it was a nightmare, they were in it together.

He patted his pocket, searching for his cell phone. It was still there. *Thank God he'd grabbed it.* He pulled it out and swiped the screen, waiting for the phone to spring to life. He kept one eye on the road as he dialed. He hit speakerphone.

The phone was silent. He dialed again, thinking he must've done something wrong, that he'd punched the numbers incorrectly.

But he hadn't.

There was no service.

The storm had probably interrupted it. Tom's cell phone reception was shoddy, even on a good day.

"Shit," he whispered.

The tires skidded over the slippery snow. The steering wheel jerked in his hands. Tom tossed the cell phone to Lorena. "Keep trying the police." Even as he said the words, he wasn't sure what the police would do.

"Okay," she said vacantly.

Tom looked over at her. Lorena's whole body was shaking, as if the gravity of what they'd seen was threatening to pull her under.

"It'll be all right, Lorena. We'll make it through this," he said, though he was far from sure. He'd spoken the words so many times over the years that they felt empty, meaningless. It was one thing losing a son to an accident.

It was another explaining *this*.

"Did you see the Smiths? Did you see what happened to Desmond and Tori?" Lorena whimpered.

"I saw them, honey. Try to calm down."

"What if they're still alive? What if we could've helped them?"

"They're dead, Lorena." Tom shook his head. "I'm sure of it. Even if they were alive, we wouldn't be able to do anything. I shot that thing in the kitchen, and it didn't stop. Did you see it? Whatever the hell these things are, we won't be able to stop them. I'm not even sure the police will."

He clenched the steering wheel, trying to quell the pit in his stomach. In spite of the irrational, *unbelievable* things they'd seen, they'd made it out alive. Somehow, they'd survived.

"Any luck with the phone?" he asked.

"Nothing," Lorena said.

"Keep trying. We're bound to have better service when we hit the main road."

He wasn't sure what calling someone would do. But they had to try, at least. He glanced over to find Lorena's teeth chattering. She was still in her pajamas. In the urgency of the moment, she hadn't had time to get dressed. Tom at least had his work clothes and boots.

"I think there's a winter jacket in the backseat," he said. "Why don't you grab it?"

Tom eyed the street in front of him. At the moment, it looked more like arctic tundra than a residential back road. He was driving on a wooded, houseless street, but eventually he'd end up on Arcadia Road, which led to a main thoroughfare.

From there, it was a fifteen-minute drive to town. In good weather, at least.

Lorena returned from the backseat. She'd located two jackets, a hat, and some boots. She handed a coat to Tom, and he unbuckled his seatbelt and wriggled into one of the jackets. When he had it on, Lorena slipped a knit hat over his head. She tried to smile, but the expression fell flat.

The SUV swayed back and forth over the road. The precipitation was deepening, and Tom had the frightening premonition that they'd be stuck and stranded. Tom scanned the white, snow-covered trees around them. Several branches lay in the road, creating obstacles for the SUV. He weaved around them with rigid, clenched hands.

The closest neighborhood was miles away. He pondered the empty houses he'd passed. He wondered if anyone else was home.

He hadn't seen a storm like this in several years, and certainly not in October. It didn't look like the plows were out. That explained the depth of the snow in the roads.

Those that had gotten out were lucky they had.

Tom shivered. Although the heat was blasting, it did little to restore the warmth to his body. They drove in silence for several minutes, Lorena checking the cell phone, murmuring in distress. Tom tried to focus on the things he could control: driving to get help, telling the authorities what they'd seen. What would he say?

He recalled Desmond's torn, mangled body. The image felt like a scene from a television show, rather than something he'd witnessed. The creatures were fit more for nightmares than reality. Would anyone *believe* him?

He pictured the beast's eyes as it had watched them through the windowpane—sizing them up, ready to burst through glass and wood if it needed to. If they'd gone to the basement, Tom had no doubt they would've been ripped apart like the others.

Desmond and Tori were dead. So were Nick and Sarah. So was everyone they'd lived alongside for the past twenty years. *They're all dead...*

Tom was so immersed in his thoughts that he almost didn't see the shadows among the trees. When he did, he stiffened.

"Oh, my God, Tom, look over there..." Lorena whispered.

The fear he'd felt at his house burrowed back inside him, clawing at his nerves. He stared out the driver's side window. The road was bordered with pine trees. White, skeletal branches protruded from the trunks, as if the limbs were trying to escape the weight of the snow.

Running among the trees were several of the beasts.

Tom kept driving, watching the creatures glide across the landscape. Every so often, one of them gazed at the road, red eyes glinting in the darkness.

"Holy shit," he said. "They're following us."

Tom hit the gas, balancing caution with the need to escape. *If we get stuck, if the vehicle dies...*

Lorena pounded frantically at the phone. The beasts increased speed, barreling closer to the road, loping on four limbs. The engine growled; the tires churned through the snow. Tom was so preoccupied with the beasts that he neglected to pay attention to what was in front of him. He swerved to the right just in time to avoid a tree branch. The road was littered with debris. The SUV tires were sturdy, but not sturdy enough to avoid a flat.

"How close are they?" he shouted.

"They're getting close, Tom! Go faster!"

Tom navigated around another branch. Sweat trickled from his forehead. In his peripheral vision, he saw several of the beasts falling over one another, as if engaged in a competition rather than hunting as a pack. He imagined them vying for the first taste of blood, anticipating the kill to come. Their growls spit from the forest.

Tom careened around several more branches in the road. Although he saw most of the obstacles in the headlights, he was worried about those he couldn't see, those that might be buried. As if to prove his point, a loud rattle tore at the undercarriage.

He grimaced and kept going.

After clearing the fallen limbs, Tom accelerated and risked a glance out the driver's side window. The beasts were falling behind. He drove for several more minutes, increasing speed as he encountered a straightaway. Soon, he'd surpassed them. Their shadows lingered in the trees and then disappeared.

He and Lorena were safe for the moment, however long the moment lasted.

He blew a nervous breath. "Check the phone again, Lorena." He tried to remain positive, but his hope waned. The snow fell harder. Even with the defroster on, the pellets clung to the windshield, gumming up his windshield wipers.

"Nothing," Lorena said.

Tom took several more turns, falling into a rhythm, focusing on the drive. The snow was deepening, and he needed to keep momentum. He traded glances between the road and the white-tipped foliage on either side of the road. For a moment, Tom was convinced they'd warped into some alternate reality, one where civilization had disappeared. He could no longer imagine anyone living here. It was as if the snow had buried the neighborhoods that once existed.

After he'd driven for several minutes, slanted rooftops pierced the skyline, patches of black fighting their way through the snow's coating. Tom stared at the buildings as if they might disappear. It took him a few seconds to recognize where he was. He was approaching Jameson Street, a street he passed every day on the way to work. Everything looked so different now.

Lorena broke his concentration. "Tom! Look out!"

Tom snapped to attention. His foot flew to the brake. Up ahead, a girl was trudging into the headlight's glow, her face pale and bruised, her clothing disheveled. He slid to a halt, pumping the brakes, coming to a stop within ten feet of her. The headlights illuminated her battered body.

"Stay here!" Tom ordered.

He grabbed his rifle and threw the vehicle into park. When he opened the door, the cold hit him at once, enveloping his body. He jumped out, leaving the door open, and ran toward the girl. The snow grabbed his ankles, trying to trip him up. The girl was trembling, injured. He was almost at her side when she collapsed. He knelt down next to her, noticing her leg was bleeding.

"Are you all right, ma'am?"

Tom helped the girl to her feet and started ushering her back to the vehicle. She didn't answer.

"Are you okay?" he asked again.

This time, some words tumbled from her mouth.

"I-I think so."

The girl was wearing sweatpants and a winter coat, but judging by her ragged breathing, she'd been out in the cold for some time. They swayed in the gust of the wind, fighting the elements, two insignificant figures against a sea of white. It was then that Tom noticed the gun in her hand. He told her to put it away. Thankfully, she complied. He asked about her leg as they narrowed the gap to the car, making their way to the rear door.

A few minutes later, the girl would tell him her name was Abby.

Half an hour later, she'd become one of *them*.

Chapter Four

Tom swallowed at the memories. Both Abby and Lorena were gone. All that was left now were he and the creatures in the forest. He concentrated on the road, gripping the steering wheel of the SUV. Snow cascaded in front of him, obscuring his view.

He'd lost the beasts, but he wasn't out of danger yet.

According to the speedometer, he was going forty miles an hour—a moderate speed for dry conditions, but a dangerous one in the snow. He'd experienced enough New England winters to realize that hitting a single patch of slippery ice or snow could cause a crash. If he crashed, that'd be the end of him. Just like it had been the end for Jeremy.

If he didn't die from the collision, he'd be torn apart by the creatures.

Tom reviewed what he knew. What he *thought* he knew.

The beasts were human. Or at least, they had been at one time. He'd seen Abby transform—her body contorting into something fit for nightmares. He'd also heard one of the creatures speak. Rob,

Abby's husband, had confessed to his killings before he'd ripped her apart.

He'd been proud of what he'd done.

Somehow the beasts had known the storm was coming. Somehow they'd sensed what was going to happen. It was as if nature had served up the perfect recipe to suit their needs, and they'd been ready to take advantage.

But none of those facts helped him now. With his empty rifle, Tom was nearly defenseless against the things.

He surveyed the landscape. The sky emptied snow.

He patted the compartment between the seats, searching for his cell phone. He was unable to contact the police before, but maybe he'd have better luck now. He located his phone and swiped the screen. The device remained dark. He tried again with no luck. *Shit.*

The battery was dead. It hadn't gotten a full charge. The power had been out for most of the night. *Remember?*

He tossed the phone on the seat, fighting a wave of hopelessness.

Stay focused, Tom.

He fought the feeling that he was alone.

Tom found it hard to imagine he was the only one left out here, but given what he'd seen, he wouldn't be surprised. It was as if some higher power had passed judgment on the world, sending its minions to rend humanity apart, one limb at a time. Tom had always lived his life in a fair manner. But the world had become a cruel, violent place.

Maybe God had finally had enough.

Tom had questioned the existence of God a lot over the past few years, especially after what had happened to Jeremy. How could a caring God take away the most important thing he had? How could a loving God put a family through so much pain? If mankind was being punished, the pieces certainly fit.

Perhaps he was truly the last man alive, condemned to this white wasteland.

Tom shook his head to clear his thoughts.

Out of nowhere, lights blazed in front of him. Tom squinted through the cracked windshield. A vehicle was stalled in the road, turned sideways in the snow, its headlights pointed into the woods. Two people in heavy coats were bent over the trunk. When they noticed Tom's SUV, they turned and waved their hands.

People! Survivors!

Tom heart leapt in his throat. A minute ago, he was convinced he was in hell, but the appearance of people reignited his hope. He caught sight of the people's faces in the headlights' glow—two frightened pairs of eyes looking at him. It looked like a young couple.

Tom slowed the SUV. The couple's vehicle had broken down in the center of the road. He took a wide berth, pulling up next to it. As he reduced speed, he fought the fear that if he stopped, he wouldn't be able to get going again. He'd take that chance.

He couldn't leave these people stranded.

He couldn't.

He swallowed his concern and rolled to a stop. Before getting out, he stared into the forest's edge. The trees were dark and looming. He unlocked the door and threw it open.

The couple was waiting for him. They trudged over to his door.

"You-you stopped," the girl said. She looked surprised.

She was wearing a thick winter coat, and the hood formed an oval around her face. Her cheeks were red, her lips were dry, and specks of blood marred her complexion. Her male companion was equally disheveled. His face was stained with grease; his coat sleeves were ripped. In spite of their tattered condition, they were alive, and they were speaking to him.

Tom's hope amplified.

"You're not going to believe it. There are these things out there—" the young man started.

Tom interrupted him. "I know, kid. Hurry and get in."

When the young couple was situated, Tom grabbed the shifter.

"What are your names?" Tom asked.

"I'm Billy, and this is my girlfriend, Ashley."

Tom felt Billy's eyes on him as he hit the gas. He turned the wheel, listening to the tires spin. After a few seconds of struggle, the car lurched forward. The girl in the backseat whimpered. It looked like she was in shock.

"Did you call the police, Billy?"

"We tried, but there's no service," Billy explained. He reached into his pants and pulled out his cell phone, as if suddenly unsure. He began swiping the screen. The kid had taken his hood off, and shaggy dark hair fell over his eyes.

Tom held out the rifle.

"Here, take this."

"Thanks, I-I guess. I've never fired a gun, though."

"Don't worry, you won't have to. It's out of ammunition. But it's all I got. It's better than nothing. If they come for us, maybe we can hit them with it."

The kid nodded, but he seemed less than relieved.

Tom maneuvered the SUV around the couple's car, kicking up snow as they progressed. Billy stared at his abandoned vehicle, as if it would spring to life and follow them.

The oncoming road was as white as the road behind them. There was no evidence that anyone had traveled it recently. The SUV was growing colder by the second. Even with the vents blasting, the heat was no match for the winter chill. The wind whistled through the bullet hole in the glass, keening through the cracked pane.

"How long have you been out here?" Tom asked.

"An hour, I think," Billy answered, his eyes wide.

"Where do you live?"

"Locust Lane. We're in the Quail Hollow Apartments. We were watching a movie when the power went out. The next thing we knew, we heard crashes from the building across the street. When we looked out the window, we saw Bill Stevenson, our neighbor, walking around his living room. And then he... he..."

The kid paused, and Tom heard him suck in a breath.

"It's okay," Tom said. "You don't have to—"

"He turned," Ashley called from the backseat. Tom's eyes switched to the rearview mirror. The girl was rocking back and forth, biting her lip. Her gloved hands were clenched together. "We saw him stagger outside. And then one of our other neighbors came outside to talk to him, to see what was going on, and he killed her. There were more things like him. Patti Laroque. Mrs. Henry. They were everywhere. They... they killed everyone in the complex..."

"I understand. We're going to get out of here, sweetheart. Don't worry."

Tom did his best to be positive, though his stomach was tangled in knots. Somewhere behind him, the creatures were watching. Biding their time. He pictured them lurking in the trees, though he couldn't see them.

He was so caught up in watching the rearview that he didn't notice the opening to a street on his left until he was upon it. The black-and-white street sign blended with the landscape, and the snow blurred any delineation between road and shoulder.

He stared down a residential road. Loomis Avenue.

In the distance he saw several houses, but no sign of people. There was a chance they'd find help in the neighborhood—a cell phone, a landline—but Tom didn't want to risk it.

If they stopped for too long, the beasts would catch up.

"Keep going..." Ashley whispered from the backseat, as if reading his thoughts.

"I won't stop until we get to town," Tom said.

"Where are we going?" Billy asked.

"The police station," Tom replied.

"There might be cops at the shelter. Or at least a place to hide."

Tom glanced at his companion, confused. "Shelter?"

"Yeah," Billy said. "Me and Ashley heard something about it on the radio. Right after the power went out, they were directing people to the Knights of Columbus."

"Really?"

"They said they had a generator. They were going to provide food and a place to sleep for the people without power. But that was before these things came out. That was the last thing we heard. I wish we'd taken the radio, but we barely got out of there in time. Maybe there'll be cops there, or at least some other people."

Tom caught a glimpse of Ashley in the backseat. She'd taken off her gloves, and she pulled at her fingertips. Blonde hair poked out of her hood at jagged angles. Her eyes were wide and vacant.

"They ate them. All of them," she whispered.

"I think she's in shock," Billy said in a low voice.

He glanced at Tom, his own face ashen.

"I don't blame her," Tom said. He sighed. "The shelter's on the way to the police station. We'll stop there first."

Billy smiled weakly. "Okay."

Tom envisioned the roads they'd have to travel. He'd lived in Plainfield his whole life; he was familiar with the layout. At the end of the two-mile road was a stoplight. Once they reached it, the Knights of Columbus was a ten-minute drive. The last time he'd been there had been for a fireman's dinner. He and Lorena had had pasta with meatballs.

The meal didn't seem quite so appetizing now.

He stared at the fuel gauge. To his relief, the SUV had a full tank of gas. If it weren't for the vehicle, he didn't know where he'd be...

Probably back in the woods, with Lorena…
Thank God we're moving.

Ashley was still rocking in the backseat, her movement visible in the rearview mirror.

"I'm going to climb in back with her. Is that okay?" Billy asked.

"I think that'd be a good idea," Tom said.

He watched as Billy climbed over the seats, taking the rifle with him. He began consoling his girlfriend.

"It'll be fine, Ash. We'll get to the shelter."

"They ate them. They ate Fred and Sylvia and Terry and…"

"I know. Try not to think about it. We're going to get help."

"I can still hear them… the way they screamed…"

"Calm down. We'll make it."

Tom swallowed. He wanted to believe the kid's words, but his faith was dissolving.

Chapter Five

The street light at the end of the road was dead and covered in snow. It swung back and forth on the wire, as if ready to give up and topple off. Tom eyed it with deepening fear. He'd expected the power to be out all over town, but the lack of life was disheartening.

The intersection was desolate, deserted.

Rather than stopping beneath the traffic light, he kept moving, afraid that a loss of speed would mean a loss of traction. As he entered the intersection, he glanced left and right out of habit, though he was certain no one was coming.

He took a right down Woodford Avenue.

Woodford was a main thoroughfare. Commercial buildings lined either side of the road, their white walls blending with the falling snow. The parking lots were empty. Several dull streetlights hung over them, as if they'd been tasked to keep vigil but had forgotten how.

Tire tracks marred the snow-covered road. They were caved in and obscured, but visible. Tom couldn't tell when they'd been made. Perhaps earlier, when others had fled the neighborhood. He followed the grooves, hoping to find better traction.

"Keep an eye on the buildings. Let me know if you see anyone," he instructed his companions. He didn't plan on stopping.

But if they were to see a cop, a survivor...

Tom traced the snow-covered buildings, searching for human presence. The doors and windows were dark. None were open; none seemed to harbor life. They passed another commercial complex, drifts of white snow clinging to the brick faces of the buildings. Big, white flakes fluttered and fell.

The moon emanated from behind the clouds.

Tom stared up at it. He recalled movies and television shows he'd seen. Were the moon and the beasts connected? The idea seemed ludicrous, insane, but he had no better answers.

They passed a warehouse on the side of the road, a bar that had been boarded and closed. Tom had driven these roads numerous times on his way to work, but he'd never paid much attention to the buildings. They were nothing more than splashes of color in the backdrop of his morning commute.

At the corner of the next intersection was a three-story factory building. This one he recognized. It was a brick building with a green garage door at the base; a partially covered sign that said "Machine Shop" adhered to the front.

He recalled seeing a pickup in the parking lot on previous trips.

It was there.

The vehicle was old and rusted. Even with the covering of snow, specks of yellow paint poked through. The lights were off in the building. But they were normally on. He stared in the windows as they passed, searching for clues as to whether it was inhabited. He surveyed each floor, scanning for signs of life. And then, right before he gave up, he saw something — a faint light moving behind one of the upper windows.

He hovered over the brake, straining for a better look. Billy interrupted him.

"Tom! Watch out!"

Tom's foot flew to the brake as something darted in front of the vehicle.

Tom saw the fur before he felt the impact. His heart jolted. He jerked the wheel, hoping to avoid the beast, but he was too late. The SUV slammed into the creature. Before Tom knew it, the vehicle was sliding on a patch of ice, skidding on the grooves he'd been riding in.

The tires locked and screeched.

Tom yelled in panic.

He tried to correct course, but couldn't — the vehicle barreled straight for a telephone pole. The hood connected with the pole, crinkling upwards. Smoke poured from the engine. Tom tried putting the vehicle into reverse, but the tires spun and spit snow, and a second later, the engine ceased.

Tom glanced out the windows. The beast was nowhere in sight.

He tried restarting the engine. Nothing.

"Where'd it go?" Ashley whimpered from the backseat.

"I don't know. I don't see it."

Tom craned his neck out the windows. He could barely feel his fingers. His nerve endings were dull from the cold; his adrenaline was firing. He turned the key into the "off" position and tried starting the car again, but the engine wouldn't turn over. The dashboard was aglow with multi-colored lights. The windows were fogged.

Billy and Ashley shifted in the backseat as they peered out the vehicle. Billy gripped the empty rifle, Ashley's head buried in his shoulder. With the engine off, the area pitched back into silence. The only sound was the *thwip* of snow against the windshield.

"Where the hell did it go?" Billy asked again.

Tom stared out the misted windows.

Billy started speaking again, but Tom silenced him. A noise had crept into earshot. Somewhere outside, an animal was whining.

The whining was shallow and high-pitched, coming from outside the passenger's side door. It sounded like the bray of something wounded, something in pain. The creature must be injured. Otherwise it'd be trying to get inside.

Right?

Tom scanned the vehicle, searching for a weapon he'd missed, but all he found was loose change, empty cans. There was nothing they could use. No way to defend themselves, other than an empty rifle and their bare hands. There was nothing except... a tire iron. He had one in back. He didn't know why he hadn't thought of it before.

"Billy," he hissed. "

"Look over the seat behind you. There should be a tire iron back there."

The kid nodded and turned in his seat. Ashley lifted her head to allow him to slip free. The blood on her face — formerly dried — was wet with tears, smeared like a Halloween mask. Tom watched Billy slide over the seat, navigating his way in back. A few seconds later, he emerged with the tire iron and passed it to Tom.

With the weapon in hand, Tom felt a little more protected, but no less afraid. The beast's whining had stopped. He glared out the passenger's side window, but the pane was fogged.

Billy and Ashley watched him from the backseat.

Tom scooted over to the passenger's seat, took a deep breath, and slowly wiped away the condensation. As the window came clean, he imagined a bestial face on the other side, glaring at him with bloodshot eyes.

What he saw was a lump of black fur lying ten feet away in the snow.

He exhaled in relief. The creature was motionless. No whining. No movement. He gave a stiff nod at the window, then turned to face Billy and Ashley.

"I think it's dead," he pronounced, quietly.

In the distance, one of the beasts howled. The noise sent a surge of dread down Tom's spine.

"Are you sure?" Billy asked. "What if it's just knocked out?"

"I can't tell," Tom admitted. "But if we stay in here, we won't last the night. They'll get to us. It's not safe in here." He pointed to the cracked, bullet-scarred windshield, the smoking engine. The creatures would find them. "We need to get out of here."

"I'm not going out there," Ashley said, her teeth chattering. "No way. Not with that *thing*."

Tom furrowed his brow and looked up at the factory building. He recalled the light he'd seen before the crash. The SUV had ended up on the side of the road, parallel to the building. The rusted pickup and the green garage door were three hundred feet away. The building might be unlocked. Either that, or maybe they'd find the keys in the pickup. It was a long shot, but they didn't have many options.

"I thought I saw something in one of the windows before we crashed," Tom said, pointing to one of the dark windows. "A light. There might be someone inside. Maybe we can find help."

He stared at the building, but the light had vanished. They had to do *something*.

"Let's go," Tom whispered.

Neither of Tom's companions moved. It was obvious they weren't going to leave, not with the beast outside. For a moment, Tom considered locking them in the SUV and venturing out for help, bringing back the police, but the image of Lorena's eviscerated body made him swallow the idea.

He couldn't leave them behind.

He needed to convince them the beast was dead, as sickening and terrifying as the idea was. He swallowed his fear and reached for the door handle.

"Wait here," he said. "I'll make sure it's safe."

He opened the door and stepped out into the cold.

PART TWO – THE FALLEN

Chapter Six

The bitter chill of the wind made Tom's eyes and nose water. His knit cap and coat were barely sufficient to brave the conditions. He wasn't even wearing gloves.

He shut the door. Somewhere behind him, Billy or Ashley engaged the locks with a click. Tom gripped the tire iron with numb hands and trudged forth, his boots like lead in the deep snow, working his way around the front of the SUV. Smoke billowed from the hood; the air reeked of engine fluids. The hood of the vehicle was melded around the telephone pole. Tom took only a cursory glance at the damage.

He had more pressing concerns.

He focused on the lump of black fur on the other side of the vehicle. It'd fallen about ten feet from the passenger's side. He peered around the hood, rabid fear gnawing his insides. He held up the tire iron, prepared to strike or to flee, whichever option seemed wiser.

The beast didn't move. The snow was stained with its blood.

Tom stared, but couldn't determine the origin or the nature of its wounds. The thing was lying facedown. Maybe they'd killed it with the SUV, and if they had, there was a good chance they could all be killed. It meant he and his companions had a chance at defending themselves.

Something flashed in his peripheral vision, and Tom's gaze roamed upwards. The light had reappeared. It was coming from one of the upper floors. The light bobbed back and forth; after a few seconds, someone shone it against the window. *Do they see us?* Tom waved his hands. His heart surged with hope.

He needed to get Billy and Ashley, and they needed to run to the building.

He gave a precautionary glance at the thing on the ground.

Only the thing wasn't there anymore. It was on its feet.

Suddenly the beast was standing fifteen feet away, glaring at Tom across the hood of the vehicle, a dark shadow in the glow of the headlights. Its eyes burned—red and rabid and full of aggression. He hadn't even heard it move. It raised its claws and opened its maw, letting out a guttural snarl.

Tom stumbled backward.

Any wounds the beast had were gone now. His mind flashed to the beast he had shot earlier that evening. How many gunshots had he fired? How many bullets had it seemed to absorb? Tom swallowed the acidic taste that crept into his throat. He took another tentative, terrified step toward the driver's door. His only hope was to get back in the car. The beast took a step of its own, matching his pace, coming toward the hood.

Inside the vehicle, something creaked. Tom heard Ashley whimpering through the glass. Were his companions watching him? Would they unlock the door? In a way, he wouldn't blame them if they didn't. The beast snarled and leapt onto the vehicle.

Tom lunged for the door handle. He grabbed it and pulled upwards, but it thudded uselessly against the doorframe. He heard Billy or Ashley unlocking it, but not in time.

The beast was already off the car and on him.

Tom smelled the thing before he felt the pain. Its breath was rancid, rotten. The beast tackled him to the snow. He sank through the deep powder and to the asphalt, clenching the tire iron.

He swung the weapon in front of him, but missed. The area around him was dark and noxious. The beast hovered over him, tearing at the snow, its claws no more than flashes in the near-darkness. He heard his coat rip. The hiss of the creature's breath. Tom cried out, but his voice was drowned out by the crazed growls of the beast.

He swung again. His blow was weak and uncoordinated, but somehow he connected with the thing's jowl. He felt something crack—its teeth, perhaps—and the thing roared and backed away. Tom struggled to right himself.

He scrambled to his feet. The beast was

standing several steps away. Tom took a defensive swing, hoping to drive it back, but it was already advancing, raising its arms. It let out a final, haunting bellow.

Tom pictured Lorena and raised the tire iron. If he were going to be killed, he'd do it on his own terms: on his feet and fighting, with the image of his wife on his mind.

A gunshot cracked across the night.

The wolf's head spattered crimson across the snow, and it dropped to the ground in front of him, coming to rest inches from his boots. Tom lowered the tire iron, terrified and confused, but *alive*. He stepped back and stared at the beast for several seconds, certain it would spring to life and resume its attack, but it remained still.

He glanced all around the snow-ridden street, trying to find the source of the explosion. Movement from the nearby building drew his eye. In one of the upper windows — the window he'd been looking at — a man was hanging out the window, a rifle tucked under his arm.

"Over here!" the man yelled, waving his arms. "Get to the garage and I'll open the door!"

The rear door of the SUV groaned and cracked open. Billy's face poked through.

"Are you all right, Tom?" Billy asked, his cheeks ashen.

"Grab Ashley! Let's go!" Tom hissed.

The door opened and Billy and Ashley spilled out onto the snow. Tom forged across the landscape, making a wide berth around the body of the fallen creature, working his way toward the building.

His pulse roared behind his ears. Just moments before, he'd been prepared to die, ready to rejoin his wife in whatever-came-after.

The fact that he was alive was a miracle.

The snow in the parking lot was deeper than the road. Tom lifted his legs above the ground, as if he were engaged in a workout. Progress was painfully slow. Several times he glanced over his shoulder at the beast, but it didn't move. Sweat slid from his knit cap and onto his brow.

The man watched them from the window. A few seconds later, he called out again.

"I'll be right down!"

Tom got a glimpse of the man in the flashlight's glow before he disappeared. He was wearing a baseball hat, and he appeared to be in his late fifties, several years older than Tom.

The window slid shut. For a second, Tom fought the dreadful feeling that they were alone, that the man would leave them stranded. But they had no other options.

They ran past the rusted pickup, the snow piled high in the bed. Tom stole a glance at the interior. He could barely see through the snow-covered windows. When they reached the green garage door, they stepped underneath an overhang, shielding their faces from the pelting snow.

Tom spun to face the parking lot. He surveyed

the open landscape, expecting to see dots of black fur on the distance, chasing them, but all he saw was the fallen body of the dead beast and the smoking SUV they'd left behind.

He glanced at Billy and Ashley. Their cheeks were red from running, their breaths hard and heavy. Billy held the empty rifle. Neither spoke.

Footsteps sounded from inside the building. The three spun to face the bay door. Tom heard the sound of gears grinding on tracks, and suddenly there was a gaping hole before him, a man standing in view. The man lowered his rifle.

"I'm Mark," he said. "Hurry up and get inside."

Chapter Seven

The man ushered them through the garage door, casting nervous glances into the parking lot. Then he lowered the door. Before it closed, Tom caught a glimpse of several industrial machines in the moon's light. He recognized them as woodworking machines. In a former life, he'd been a cabinetmaker. Before he could study the rest of the room, the room went black.

Tom had a moment of anxiety.

He didn't know this man or what his intentions were. What if Mark attacked them—or worse? Tom reached out to confirm Billy and Ashley's whereabouts. The girl startled.

"It's all right. It's just me," Tom said. "I'm just making sure we're all here."

He clutched the tire iron, just in case.

A flashlight flicked on. Mark shined it on each of them, his eyes roving between them. His face was backlit in the glow, allowing Tom a better look at him. The man was sporting a *Titleist* baseball cap and a day's worth of stubble.

"I was watching out the window," he said. "I saw you guys crash back there."

"Thanks for shooting that thing," Tom replied.

"I probably would've died if you hadn't. But how'd you—?"

"Not now. We need to get upstairs. There'll be more coming, after all the noise we've made. I hope they didn't see the light."

Mark gave them a hard stare and then changed direction, heading further into the building. Tom paused for a second, enough to verify Billy and Ashley were next to him, and then followed the bobbing light through the room. Mark moved fast. Tom struggled to keep up, skirting industrial machines and boxes, objects that were little more than silhouettes in the backlight of the flashlight. The air was dank and cold, but less frigid than outside. When they reached the edge of the room, Mark disappeared through a doorway and mounted a stairwell. Tom glanced over his shoulder, fearful that he'd find the garage door open and vicious, slavering beasts on their tail.

The room remained dark.

They forged up the stairs, Mark pointing the flashlight over his head, as if they were miners in a cavern, exploring the twists and turns of some long-forgotten ruins. The staircase was steep and wooden, and Tom concentrated on quieting his footsteps as they walked. No matter how many walls and doors they hid behind, he didn't feel safe.

He'd never feel safe again.

When they reached the third floor, Mark paused at a doorway, using a key to unlock a wide, wooden door. He opened it and stuck his gun through the entrance. He scrutinized the room before proceeding. Then he led Tom, Billy, and Ashley into a room that smelled of grease and sawdust.

Once they were inside, Mark locked the door.

"Help me barricade the door," he said to Tom, shining the flashlight on an industrial saw that looked like it'd been used for that purpose.

Tom set his tire iron on top of the machine, then unlocked the wheels and rolled the machine in place. When the door was secure, they paused to catch their breath. Mark wiped his face with his sleeve.

"Thanks for letting us in," Ashley said, breaking the silence.

Mark nodded. He eyed each of them in the pale glow of the flashlight. His eyes were ringed and bloodshot; it looked like he hadn't slept in days.

"What's going on out there?" Tom asked.

Mark cleared his throat. "Damned if I know," he said.

He avoided their eyes as he walked toward an open window across the room. The room was square, about fifty feet wide and long. Tom, Billy, and Ashley followed him, dodging tables and machinery that adorned the floor space. A row of large windows lined the opposite wall, allowing moonlight to seep into the room's edges. The windowsills were only a few feet off the ground.

Before Tom could get acquainted, Mark switched off the flashlight.

"We need to call the police," Tom said.

"Can't. Phone lines are dead," Mark said. "I tried."

"Do you have a cell phone?"

"A prepaid. I left it at home. I don't use it much, anyway. I mostly use the landline." Mark reached out, swung the window inwards, and latched it closed. Tom assumed it was where he'd fired at the beast.

"What do you think we should do?" Tom asked.

"Stay here and wait out the storm. Even if we got a hold of someone, no one would know what to do with these things."

"What are they?" Tom asked.

Mark hunkered by the window, but didn't answer. Did he know more than he let on?

Tom walked across the room, keeping his voice low. "I saw people changing into them," he said. "A man and a woman, they *transformed*. These things are human underneath."

"I know that already. Look." Mark crouched next to one of the windows and pointed. Tom hunkered beside him and followed his hand. Across the parking lot, Tom saw his crumpled SUV wrapped around the telephone pole, the headlights blazing. Next to it was the barely-clothed body of a human. It took him a second to realize it was the creature who'd attacked him earlier.

"You killed it."

"That wasn't the first one, either." Mark adjusted his rifle.

"I don't understand. I shot one of them an hour ago. I put six goddamn bullets in the thing, and it barely wounded it. In fact, I'm pretty sure it even—"

"Healed?" Mark asked, his eyes wide and manic.

"Yes. How'd you know that?"

"Because that's what happened when I shot one for the first time."

"What do you mean?"

"I didn't use the ammunition my brother gave me, and the thing got back up and attacked me. But I've wizened up since then."

"I don't understand."

"I should've listened to my brother. I should've listened to Colton." Mark reached into his coat pocket and pulled out a handful of bullets. He held them next to the window, allowing the glare to capture the silver surface. "If I'd used these the first time, I wouldn't have had a problem. I won't make that mistake again."

Tom felt an inkling of something he'd known before. Something he *should've* known. And yet he'd refused to believe it. Couldn't believe it. Things like this shouldn't be happening in the real world, not outside the realm of fantasy and television. For the second time that night, he entertained the idea that he was dreaming, that the entire night had been an elaborate hoax. But the chill in his bones and the cold fear in his stomach told him it was real. And so did the body outside, lying in the snow.

Mark replaced the ammunition in his pocket and stared out the window, his rifle tucked rigidly under his arm.

"Where's your brother now?" Tom asked.

"He's dead," Mark answered.

Tom's fear was replaced with pity. Up until now, Mark had seemed hard, calloused. Uncaring. But now he understood why. He recalled Lorena's gutted body in the forest, his guilt at leaving her behind. He lowered his eyes. "Did they get to him?"

"No. I did." Mark stared over at him, his eyes lit by the moonlight. "He was one of them. I had to kill my brother."

Chapter Eight

Tom, Billy, and Ashley drew back in shock. Mark watched out the window in silence for a minute, ensuring the landscape was quiet. Then he began speaking. His voice was eerily calm, despite the tale he told.

"My brother's name was Colton. For the past twenty years, we've owned this machine shop," Mark said. "It was passed down to us from our father. About a year ago, Colton started behaving strangely. He started telling me he was having strange dreams. Violent dreams. In these dreams, he did awful things to people, and he was unable to stop himself. He felt sick about it. I told him he shouldn't worry about it; plenty of people had nightmares."

Mark readjusted.

"After a while, I got the feeling Colton might've actually done these things. One day I asked him point blank. Colton started to cry. He told me he'd done *all* of it, but that it wasn't him. That something else had taken him over; had *changed* him."

"Like the things outside," Ashley whispered.

"Yes, but not quite. A year earlier, he explained, he'd met a woman at a bar. They'd hit it off and he'd taken her to a hotel. They were both drunk. He and the woman were on the bed together when the woman bit him. She ripped a chunk from his shoulder. Colton threatened to go to the police, but she pleaded with him not to. He kicked her out of the room."

"Later that night, Colton started feeling sick. He was lying in the motel room, unable to sleep, when he started convulsing. Colton managed to get to the bathroom, but he thought he was dying. His body started… changing. His limbs stretched. He tried to hold it back, but it felt like something was inside of him, trying to get out. When he looked in the mirror, he saw what he'd become, and he went into shock. He collapsed on the floor and blacked out."

"The next morning, Colton woke up covered in blood. It wasn't his. He knew he'd done something horrible, but at the same time, he knew he'd be locked up, whether he remembered it or not."

Mark cleared his throat quietly. He stared out the window while he talked.

"The change kept happening. Colton started handcuffing his wrist to the bed at night, thinking he could control himself, but when he woke up, the cuffs were on the floor and he was covered in remains. Eventually, he started remembering things. The memories made it impossible for him to focus. He started drinking nightly. One night, a few months after the first incident, he ran into the same woman at the bar."

"They got to talking; they ended up at the hotel again. Colton was so intoxicated he'd probably forgotten what she'd done. He told her everything. He confessed all the things he'd done, everything that had happened. Instead of being terrified, the woman smiled and told him that she was the one who'd changed him. That she'd seen something in him." Mark swallowed. "That's why she'd bitten him. That's why she'd turned him into what he was. She told him what he'd become. What they all are."

"What are they?" Tom asked, afraid to hear the answer.

"They're wolves, Tom. Lycans." The light of the window illuminated enough of Mark's face to tell he was serious.

"How did your brother react?"

"He went into a fit of rage, screaming at the woman to fix what she'd done. But there was no going back. She told him he was a coward, that she'd made a mistake in turning him. And then she left and he never saw her again."

Tom gazed outside the window, as if speaking about the creatures would somehow call them to the building. He shook his head in disbelief. The story confirmed everything that had happened. For the past few hours, the rational part of his brain had been in constant battle with his senses, trying to disprove what he was seeing. But Mark's story gave it a layer of truth.

"So... You said you killed him?" Billy asked

after a moment, breaking the quiet. The young man leaned forward, listening attentively.

"After he confessed, he wanted me to. He said there were more like him. He'd seen them in the night; he'd even talked to a few of them. He told me he'd already tried to kill himself, but couldn't. It was like the beast inside him wouldn't allow it." Mark patted his coat pocket. "He gave me the bullets I showed you, but I wouldn't hear of doing that to him. He said he had a whole stash of bullets at home, and that I should use them to protect myself. I told him he was crazy. I still didn't believe him, you understand. I didn't want to feed his delusions."

"What happened?" Tom asked.

Mark shook his head sadly. "We tried to move past it. Colton stopped talking about it as much. But he continued drinking. A few days ago, he warned me that I wouldn't be able to ignore it much longer. He said a storm was coming, that all the beasts were waiting for it. A bunch of them had migrated to the northeast in preparation, he said. It was one of the few times they could kill without fear, without repercussion. They all knew it was coming, like they sensed it in the air or something. While man was preoccupied, they'd feast, he said. They called it The Great Storm."

A cold terror gripped hold of Tom. He turned to look in the darkness behind him, as if the machines themselves would spring to life, but the room stayed silent and still.

"What happened to Colton?" Billy asked.

Mark shook his head. "Earlier today, while Colton and I were working, he made me promise to keep an eye on him. He said we should lock ourselves in here tonight. He was crying. I promised to do it. I still didn't believe him, you understand. I thought this whole thing was a hallucination, and after tonight he'd have no choice but to get help. So I locked all the doors. And then the storm hit. Everything was fine, at first, and then he… he turned. His whole body, his whole face…"

"Where is he now?" Billy whispered.

Mark raised his arm and pointed across the room. His eyes glistened with tears in the pale light of the window. "He's in that storage room. I killed him. And when this is over, I'm going to bury him where he'll never be found."

Chapter Nine

Tom stared across the room at the door. Billy and Ashley inched backward.

"Don't worry," Mark assured them. "He's dead. I made sure of it. Colton's finally at peace."

The door was little more than an outline in the dark. Tom fought the fear that the man-beast would come bursting from inside, rending them to pieces. Mark had already confessed to killing his brother, but Tom had never considered the dead man might be so close.

Mark patted the rifle in his lap. "Colton was right about everything. After he turned, he came at me like I was nothing, like we weren't even blood. I shot him several times, but he kept coming. I finally locked myself in that storage room. That's where I'd stashed the bullets he gave me. If I hadn't found them, I'd be dead right now." Mark swallowed.

The group peered through the window, watching wind kick up the snow outside.

"So what do we do?" Ashley whispered.

Mark sighed. "I have a feeling if we wait out this storm, we'll be all right. That's what Colton said. According to my brother, the beasts only hunt by the light of the moon. This storm has significance. They knew it was coming; they've been waiting for it. They knew most of us wouldn't be prepared." He pointed to the sky outside, where the outline of the moon hung behind the storm clouds. "I think it's something in their blood that tells them what's coming, kind of like animals sensing a change in barometric pressure. They've detected the storm for a while. Their senses are like animals, only much more heightened."

Tom thought back to a few hours earlier, when he'd stared at the moon through his basement window. If only he'd understood what it meant. If he had, maybe Lorena would still be alive.

But how could he have?

Tom gripped the tire iron and glanced back at Billy, who was still carrying the empty rifle. If they were going to survive the storm, they'd need to be prepared.

"Are there any other weapons in here?" he asked Mark.

Mark shook his head. "I have some tools. But they won't be much defense against the things. The only thing I'm sure of is this." He held up his rifle. "Why don't we load yours with the ammunition I have left? Is that a 22?"

Tom nodded. "Yes, it's an older one. With a tubular magazine."

Billy handed over the rifle, and Mark loaded it with the remaining bullets he'd gotten from Colton. He handed the weapon to Tom. When Mark was finished, there were six rounds in the gun — not enough to make Tom feel safe, but definitely an improvement.

"I should've listened and taken the rest of Colton's ammunition." Mark sighed. "But I didn't want to acknowledge what he was saying. I thought I was helping him by ignoring him."

"Where does he live?"

"Over on Chestnut Street. Number twenty-three. It's a yellow house at the end of the cul-de-sac, a good eight miles away on the other side of town. He said his basement was filled with supplies."

"Dammit."

"If we were closer, we might have a chance at getting them. But I don't think we should risk going out there. I think we're better off hunkering down in here." Mark set the flashlight on the floor next to him.

Tom recalled how he'd seen the light earlier, and felt a surge of gratitude.

"I saw the light before we crashed," Tom said.

"I was trying to signal you," Mark explained. "I saw the creature coming up behind you and knew you'd need help. Thank God it worked out."

"I appreciate it," Tom said again. "If you hadn't shot that thing, I don't know where we'd be."

The group fell silent, listening to the keening wind and the creak of the old building. The air grew colder by the minute. Without the distraction of conversation, Tom felt the chill of the building working through his joints, numbing his fingers and toes. He was gloveless. His boots were filled with ice.

He stared out the frosted windows, taking in the parking lot and the road. Spirals of smoke still wafted from the SUV. The dead man-beast lay nearby. The body was covered in a thin layer of snow, partially buried by the elements. Tom wondered how long it would take until the man was fully covered.

The parking lot across the street was deep and wide and filled with snow. The buildings were lifeless. Tom stared at each of them as if for the first time. The storm had painted them with a thick white brush. All of them looked the same. Tom's eyes started to glaze. The longer he stared, he started seeing things: creatures in every doorway, faces in every grime-covered window. He blinked to rid himself of the images.

After a few moments, he peered into the room behind him, acquainting himself with the building. He recalled the stairs they'd traveled to get here.

"How many floors are in this building? Three?" he whispered to Mark.

"Yes. We're on the top floor," Mark affirmed.

"How many exits?"

"Four—two in the back, one on the side, and one in the front. I blocked all of them after what happened to Colton. The only way out is the way you came in. I left the garage unblocked so I could get to my truck as a last resort."

"Do you think it'll drive if we need it?"

"Not likely." Mark gave a grim smile, his stubble-covered face illuminated by the light of the window. "That truck is hard to start on a good day. I don't think it'd get far in this weather. Besides, driving a vehicle out there is the equivalent of wearing a bull's-eye."

Tom nodded, noting his downed SUV. Even his vehicle—newer and more reliable than the truck—had barely navigated the deep snow. Mark was probably right. The best option was to stay put. If they could outlast the storm, someone would drive by eventually. Help would come.

It *had* to come.

They hung near to the window, keeping a watchful eye but maintaining their distance. Out of the corner of his eye, Tom saw Billy hugging Ashley, assuring her things would be all right.

He hoped to God it was true.

After an uneventful half hour, movement up the road drew Tom's attention. He readied his gun. The group tensed—a series of gasps and rustled coats. A vehicle was approaching in the distance, coming from the same direction they'd traveled. At the moment, it was several blocks away. He pictured a police car bursting onto the scene, ready to provide assistance. But it wasn't a cruiser. It was a pedestrian vehicle. The car weaved back and forth over the snow as if it were a ship on rough water, its dark paint illuminated by the moon's glow. It was a station wagon with two occupants.

A pit grew in Tom's stomach.

"What do we do?" whispered Ashley. "Should we signal them?"

She scurried over and grabbed Mark's flashlight, prepared to turn it on. Mark reached over and stopped her. "No. Don't," he warned. "Look."

He pointed out the window. In the time they'd been watching, a pack of furred shadows had emerged from a building near the station wagon. They barreled at the car with remarkable speed, cutting across the snow as if it were dry, flat pavement. The station wagon swerved; the occupants screamed in the distance.

At the moment, the beasts were little more than black objects on the white landscape. They were almost at the car.

"Oh, God!" Ashley slapped her hand over her mouth. "We have to do something!"

Tom's heart sputtered. He sprang for the closest window and fiddled with the latch. He wasn't sure how he could help, but he needed to do *something*. He unlocked the window and pushed it open, letting in a rush of cold air, sticking his gun through the crevice. He aimed. He wasn't the best shot — he hadn't hunted in years — but maybe he could ward the things off. Worst case, maybe he could distract them.

Mark pushed open the window next to him, taking a similar position.

But the beasts were too far away.

Tom swiveled his sights from the one creature to the next, but they were well out of range. In mere seconds, they'd enveloped the car. Several sprang on the hood, raking and clawing at the exterior. A few pounded the windows. Tom recalled his encounter in the SUV. It felt like he was watching an alternate reality, a twisted replay of the fate he'd almost endured.

He felt hopeless and powerless.

Growls and commotion filled the air. A window shattered. The station wagon veered off the road and into a building, the occupants screaming. The beasts were already pulling them out of the car. Tom prepared to fire, hoping he could distract the things, but Mark stopped him.

"Don't shoot," Mark hissed, voice trembling. "We'll only draw their attention. It's too late."

"But we can't just—" Tom trembled and lowered the gun, knowing Mark was right.

The two occupants were thrust into the snow. The beasts clawed at their bodies, dragging pieces of flesh and clothing across the landscape. The people flailed, squirmed, and finally stopped moving. The creatures buried their faces in the carnage and feasted.

Tom drew back from the window, covering his mouth with his hand. He resisted the urge to be sick. In just seconds, the wintry scene was awash in blood. Ashley cried into Billy's shoulder, her quiet gasps filling the room.

"Be quiet," Mark managed, his own voice quivering. He leaned over and closed his window, beckoning Tom to do the same. They latched them silently.

Tom lowered his gun and put his head in his hands.

"There was nothing we could've done," Mark reassured him.

Tom gritted his teeth. Over the course of the night, he'd seen more bloodshed than he had in his lifetime: Lorena, Abby, and now these people. It was as if some cruel god was piling on the tragedy, seeing how much he could take.

And the worst part was, it was far from over.

Chapter Ten

The beasts feasted for several minutes, reveling in the gore they'd created. The station wagon bore silent witness. From a distance, the scene felt surreal, as if Tom were observing a cable show documentary rather than witnessing something in front of him. He swallowed. The gory remains of the station wagon's occupants could just as easily have been them, had they been outside.

The wind snarled, rattling the windows, misting Tom's view of the scene. When it finally cleared, the beasts had finished their meal. Almost in unison, they spread out across the landscape, heads swiveling in all directions, eyes scouring the street. Several darted for the SUV. Tom's pulse spiked. He watched as they closed the gap with incredible speed, loping on furred, inhuman legs. If he hadn't known better, he would've insisted they'd never been human—creatures that had originated in some faraway place, rather than on Earth.

His eyes roamed to the body by the SUV. The man had sunk further into the snow, but pieces of him remained uncovered. Within seconds the beasts were hovering over him, inspecting the ground. They glanced from the SUV to the body then back again. For a moment, Tom was certain they were constructing the story from the snow. Did they have the ability to reason? Did they have the ability to discern what had happened?

They raised their heads, extended their snouts into the air, and sniffed.

They looked at the building.

Tom and his companions ducked, their breathing rapid and fearful. Tom stared at a spot below the windowsill, his gaze unmoving, as if the slightest bit of motion would draw the creatures near. He listened for any clue as to what the creatures were doing, but heard nothing. The wind gusted. The building creaked. Tom realized he was sweating. Despite the chill in the air, his heart was pounding furiously, warming his upper body. He glanced over at Mark. The man's face was fraught with fear.

After a few torturous moments, Tom clutched the windowsill and pulled himself up. He peered through the glass, inspecting the world an inch at a time. He saw the buildings across the street. The snow blanketed road. The SUV. No sign of the creatures. Where were they? His gaze wandered to the station wagon, then to the opposite end of the road. Nothing.

"Are they gone?" Ashley whispered.

Her words were so meek that for a moment Tom was sure he was imagining them. It wasn't until she asked again that he answered.

"I think so," he said.

One by one his companions resumed their positions. The world outside had returned back to what it was, with the exception of the bloodied bodies and the station wagon.

"Hey, wait a minute," Mark said. "The one I killed is gone."

Tom studied the area by the SUV. Mark was right. The man's body had vanished.

"Where the hell is it?" Tom whispered. He scoured the ground but saw no sign of it.

"Maybe they cleaned up after themselves," Billy offered. "Maybe they're getting rid of the evidence."

"What about the cars? The bodies?" Mark asked.

"I bet they're protecting their own."

Billy's words sent a shudder down Tom's spine. They suggested a level of cunning that was almost as frightening as the beast's primordial nature. He swallowed the thought.

They watched in silence for several minutes, the only sound the occasional creak of their boots. The wind blew in intermittent gusts, rerouting the falling snow. In another scenario, the authorities would arrive soon to take control of the scene, snapping photographs and tagging remains.

The isolation reigned.

A long, triumphant howl sounded in the distance.

Tom considered the way the beasts had torn into the station wagon, the way they'd shattered the windows and ripped the people from inside. "Is there anything else we can use to block the door?" he asked Mark. "Do you think that table saw is enough?"

"We can push a lathe in front of it. Maybe stack some boxes."

"Let's do it." Tom backed away from the window and motioned to Billy and Ashley. "Stay here and keep watch."

He made his way across the room, following Mark's shadowed form. The industrial machines hung like statues in the dark, forcing him to weave around them. Tom only had a vague sense of what the room looked like in the light. The building was as much a mystery to him as the creatures outside. In another situation, he might've been intimated by the darkness, but now he was grateful for the cover.

After walking a few steps, Mark winked on his flashlight and played the beam across the floor, illuminating the machine they'd placed in front of it earlier. The door was wooden and seemed sturdy, but Tom knew better than to trust it. They walked to a nearby corner.

"Help me stack those boxes," Mark said, shining the light to a nearby corner. Tom retrieved several, helping Mark carry and stack them. They piled them on top of the machine, covering the top half of the door. Then they moved another machine behind the first. This one didn't have wheels, and was more difficult to move. They grunted as they slid it across the floor.

When they were finished, Tom wiped the dust onto his jeans. His heart hammered against his ribcage; his body was sweating from the exertion, but it felt good to keep busy. Anything to keep from dwelling on the bloodshed he'd seen outside. He caught his breath and peered back across the room at the windows. Billy and Ashley's frames were silhouetted against the snow. Billy had his arm around the girl. To a casual observer, they might be mistaken for a young couple admiring the first snow.

Mark watched them, as well.

"Are they your neighbors?"

"Technically. But I've never met them. Their car stalled on Arcadia and I picked them up."

"They're lucky you stopped."

Tom nodded solemnly. "If you call that luck. It's awful, what they've had to witness."

"They don't have any other family close by?"

"I don't think so. At least, none that they mentioned."

"I don't know if that makes things worse or better," Mark said. "The thought of losing any more family is terrible."

"I know what you mean." Tom shook his head grimly.

"Do you live alone, Tom?"

"No. I was with my wife." Tom struggled to

keep his emotions at bay. "I lost her on the way here. She was killed by one of them."

"I'm so sorry," Mark said. He scuffed the ground with his boot. "I'm glad you made it, though. We're going to get through this, Tom."

Mark patted his shoulder. Tom agreed and stared across the room at the window. The moon shone bright through the clouds. Its presence was like a spectral warning, commanding they stay hidden.

Another hour passed. Or what Tom guessed was an hour. He resumed his position next to the window, keeping an uneasy vigil next to his companions. Ashley barely moved. She tucked her head in Billy's arm, cloaking her face from the landscape outside. Tom was worried about her mental state. Were it not for the occasional sound of her breathing, he might've thought the girl was injured, maybe even dead. Billy drew nervous breaths of his own. Every so often, he checked on his girlfriend.

"Are you two holding up all right?" Tom whispered.

"I wish we'd made it to the shelter," Billy admitted. "If that thing hadn't run out in front of us, maybe we would've gotten to the police."

"I know. But at least we're safe for the moment. There's no way to know if anyone's even there. We'll find help in the morning. I'm sure of it."

Billy nodded, his face still troubled. Tom changed the subject.

"How long have you two lived in town?" he asked, as much to distract himself as to distract the couple.

"About a year," Billy answered. "We moved out of our parents' houses and got an apartment together. We're from West Hartford."

"How long have you been dating?"

"Two years—since senior year in high school. We met in Chemistry."

"I was never good at Chemistry." Tom smiled.

"Me neither." Billy laughed nervously. "Ashley used to help me with my homework."

At the sound of her name, Ashley poked her head from beneath Billy's arm and glanced at Tom. Her face was still ashen, but Tom thought he detected a faint smile.

"Billy would buy me dinner every time he passed a test."

Tom laughed softly. "That's a nice way to get to know each other. Are you both in college?" he asked.

"We're at Tunxis Community. But we're saving to transfer to Central Connecticut."

Tom eyed the couple, his thoughts drifting to Jeremy. Jeremy had always done well in school. He'd even tutored several students in the younger grades. If Jeremy had still been alive, he would've been finishing college about now.

Tom sighed and turned back to the window.

Outside, the flakes continued to fall. The SUV had stopped smoking; the hood was covered in a layer of white. The depth of the snow seemed to have doubled. Tom measured the precipitation by the tires of the SUV, which seemed to be sinking into the landscape.

He looked back at the station wagon. The occupants were half-buried next to it, their remains painted white by the storm. He made a mental note of where they'd fallen. If and when he got out of here alive, he'd communicate those details to the police.

Tom wondered if others were hunkered nearby. Certainly, others must be doing the same things they were. Not everyone could've been killed so fast.

He imagined a roomful of people on their haunches, nervously anticipating the end. Maybe even in a building nearby.

Billy tugged his arm.

"I see something!" Billy hissed.

Tom followed his gaze to a building diagonal from the machine shop. The building was the same height as the one they were in—it contained three floors and a wealth of windows. Billy was pointing at the floor across from them. To Tom's surprise, a light was flickering behind one of the panes. Tom saw the outline of a face.

"Is that a woman?"

Tom squinted, wondering if he was seeing things, but clearly, Billy saw the woman, too.

The woman moved, her face little more than a reflection in the glass. Tom, Mark, Billy, and Ashley hunched over the windowsill, their noses fogging up the windowpanes as they tried to get a better look. From a distance of about five hundred feet, the woman's face was little more than a featureless oval. Tom pressed his hand against the glass, trying to capture the woman's attention.

Was she signaling them?

Maybe she'd already contacted the police.

A ripple of hope made its way through the others. Soon they were all waving at the woman. Her head swiveled. Tom caught a glimpse of a pink winter jacket in the dim, flickering light.

"Does she see us?" Ashley asked, pressing her own hands against the pane. She reached out as if she could touch the lady.

"I'm not sure," Tom said.

"Over here!" Billy mouthed.

The woman's head swayed back and forth over the building, then over the lifeless landscape. It looked like she was in a trance. Tom set down his rifle and joined his companions in waving. He desperately wanted to run outside, to get to her, but he'd never make it. In a night filled with violent, snarling creatures, a few hundred feet might as well be a mile.

"Keep the noise to a minimum," Mark warned, "We don't want to alert any of those things."

Billy and Ashley quieted down. Tom stared at

the woman. He wondered if she'd witnessed the same things they had.

Maybe she'd seen worse.

"I have an idea," Ashley said.

Before anyone could ask what it was, Ashley snatched the flashlight and flicked it on. She waved it at the window. "Hello!" she cried, her demeanor emboldened by the light.

"Shut that off!" Mark hissed, trying to grab it, but Ashley pulled the flashlight away.

"Hold on a second! She sees us!" Ashley said.

The woman held her lighter closer to the window. She pressed her face against the glass, shouting words they couldn't hear. She'd seen them.

"We have to get to her! She needs help!" Ashley urged, her voice a blend of nervousness and excitement.

Mark made another grab for the flashlight. This time he caught hold of it. He tugged it away and shut it off, grunting in anger.

Tom shook his head. "We can't run out there blindly. It's too dangerous."

The woman continued to wave; after a few seconds, she tried to open the window. It was stuck. The woman pointed across the street at them, then at herself. Then she ducked from view.

"What's she doing?" Billy asked.

A sudden pang of fear hit Tom's gut.

"I think she's coming over," Tom said. He held his palms flat against the window, as if to warn the woman. "Stay put!" he whispered softly, as if she might hear him.

But it was too late. The woman was gone.

Billy and Ashley panicked, the ripple of hope turning to panic. Mark opened one of the windows and held his rifle over the sill. Tom followed suit. He studied the entrance of the building, praying the woman would smarten up and stay inside. The landscape was calm. Alluring.

Don't go out there, he shouted internally.

"Keep an eye on the road," Mark hissed, his rifle swaying back and forth. "If she comes out, we have to cover her."

Tom's heart hammered. He squinted as he studied the landscape, prepared to fire at the first sign of trouble. The front door of the building moved. A patch of snow fell off the top of the door, cascading to the ground.

"Dammit. Here she comes," Mark hissed.

Tom squinted and kept his aim. He saw the sleeve of a coat, the pale glow of a lighter. It looked like she was peering out into the street. He recalled what had happened to the station wagon's occupants. They hadn't had a chance. The creatures had swarmed them in seconds. This woman would be even more vulnerable — on foot and alone, without a car to protect her.

As soon as the woman emerged, he'd shout at her. He'd do what it took to keep her safe.

Before he got the chance, something banged on the garage door downstairs, startling them.

"What was that?" Ashley cried.

Tom looked into the darkness behind them, then back outside. "I'm not sure."

"It couldn't be the woman. She hasn't even come out yet," Mark said, his voice shaking.

The banging came again—louder and more violent this time. It sounded like the garage door was buckling. Mark stuck his head out the window, inspecting the ground below them, and then leaned back inside. He swung his rifle in front of him.

"Shit!" he hissed. "We have bigger problems. They've found us!"

PART THREE – THE ATTACK

Chapter Eleven

Tom, Mark, Billy, and Ashley hunkered by the windows, listening to the crashing sounds below them.

"How many are there?" Tom asked.

"I can't tell!" Mark's voice wavered. "At least five! Maybe more!"

Tom stood and turned toward the window he'd opened, the cold air rifling against his face. He stuck his gun outside. The ground was fifty feet below. For a brief moment, he feared one of the beasts might leap up and pull him from his perch. The thought was unreasonable, and yet, after everything he'd seen, nothing seemed out of the question.

He braced his knees against the windowsill and leaned outward. The beasts were mashed up against the building in a frenzy. He heard claws tearing at the garage, the heaves of animals that knew what was on the other side. The things piled over each other in a barrage of limbs, clusters of black fur moving faster than Tom could imagine. He gritted his teeth and took aim.

He fired.

The bullet punctured one of the creatures—a furred arm, a face, a torso—he wasn't sure, but the ensuing howl made him recoil, as if the sound itself might attack him. The beast fell to the ground, creating a hole in the pack. Four others looked up. They stared at him with red eyes, snapping and snarling. He took aim at another and fired, but missed. The bullet ripped into the snow.

Movement to his left snagged his attention. Mark was leaning out the adjacent window. The man fired a round of his own, striking another of the things. The creature toppled to the ground, spraying fluid. It didn't get up. The remaining beasts growled and scattered, racing to the other side of the building and loping out of view.

Tom held his position at the window. His eyes wandered to the fallen beasts. He felt some small sense of satisfaction, though he knew it wouldn't last. He looked over at Mark.

"The bullets work," he said.

"Yes. But we're going to run out of ammunition soon," Mark warned. His face was pale in the moonlight. "Save what you have."

As if on cue, a series of bangs erupted from the rear of the building. A pit formed in Tom's stomach. Despite his hope, they hadn't scared the things off—they'd merely redirected them. He and Mark ducked back into the building.

"How stable are the doors downstairs?" Tom asked.

"I barricaded them as best as I could. But I don't think it'll stop them for long. Not after what we've seen."

Crashes echoed around the neighborhood, bouncing off the adjacent walls. With the neighborhood silent, each thud took on a life of its own, reverberating off walls and alleys. The noise was as terrifying as the beasts—it signified they were closing in.

Tom glanced across the street, searching for the woman they'd seen earlier. In the hysteria of the moment, he'd forgotten her. The parking lot was empty. The door had closed.

But in the distance, he heard screaming. He surveyed the building. It took him a second to determine the windows had been smashed.

No. Not her, too.

Movement drew his attention. More beasts emerged on the horizon. Creatures appeared from alleyways and corners, speckling the landscape black. Their snarls carried with the wind. They converged on the building as if it were a single entity, a fresh carcass fit for consumption.

Tom gritted his teeth and repositioned at the window. The moon's pale glow seeped into the room. Out of the corner of his eye, he saw Billy holding his tire iron into the air, threatening the shadows around them. Ashley clung to him for support.

"We'll never last in here," she whispered.

The realization hit Tom like a punch to the stomach. Even though they'd killed several of the beasts—as encouraging as that was—there was no way they could take them all. Sooner or later the things would get inside. He clenched the rifle in his hand, envisioning the four remaining bullets inside. Mark had six, by his count.

How far would the bullets go?

He felt trapped. Caged. It was the way he'd felt back at his house, knowing that reprieve was only temporary. He glanced down, surveying the fifty-foot drop to the ground—much too high to consider jumping without serious injury.

That was a last resort.

A crash emanated from downstairs. Tom heard the sound of glass shattering, objects being trampled. The beasts were inside.

"Over by the entrance!" Mark yelled, pulling Tom's arm. "We need to get a clear shot once they get to the door! We need to hold them back!"

"What about us?" Billy asked frantically, holding up his tire iron.

"Stay put."

"I want to help!" Billy arched his back. He wielded the tire iron with bravado, even though Tom could tell he was afraid.

"You should hunker down," Tom said. "Protect Ashley."

The girl was clutching her boyfriend's arm, her body wracked with fear.

"Why don't you go in there?" Mark shouted, pointed at the storage room.

"No way. We're not going in there with that thing," Billy said. "No offense."

Tom swallowed. The banging downstairs had

grown to a crescendo. Ashley pulled Billy's arm, her face contorted with fright.

"Let's go, Billy! We have to hide."

"But what if that thing is—"

"I'll bring you over," Tom said, wielding his rifle. "Come on!" He collected Billy and Ashley and instructed her to bring the flashlight.

Mark ran toward the barricaded door, skirting machines and tables, while Tom led the frightened kids toward the eastern end of the room. Ashley winked on the flashlight and shined it at the storage room, sniffling as she ran. When they reached the door, Tom raised his gun and sucked in a breath. He threw it open.

Mark's brother, Colton, lay on the floor, his naked body marred with bullet holes. His eyes were wide and staring at the ceiling. The room smelled of copper, sweat, and animal musk.

Tom lowered his gun. Whatever Colton had been was gone. Tom ushered Billy and Ashley in the room and told them to stay quiet. They complied, sidestepping past the body and further into the room.

"Stay put until I come get you," Tom said.

"What if you don't?" Ashley asked, her eyes frantic.

"I will," Tom said simply.

He shut the door without a word, hit with a needle of guilt. There was no time to consider it further. The crashing in the building was getting closer. The things were making their way through the lower level. He flew through the room, leading with the gun. He saw Mark's outline by the door, silhouetted by the moonlight. He wove past several machines, bumping unseen objects on his way over.

He reached his new companion and took aim at the door, staring at the shadows of the machines they'd used to block it. Growls emanated from the bowels of the building. The moon lanced through the windows.

"Get ready," Mark whispered. "They're getting near the stairs."

Tom swallowed. He wasn't even close to ready.

But he had no choice but to prepare.

Chapter Twelve

Mark gritted his teeth. He stared at the door. The noises from the building's basement froze his blood, but in more ways than he let on. His conscience was riddled with guilt. Everything he'd told Tom, Billy, and Ashley was true. He hadn't made up a single bit of it.

The only thing he'd held back was the bite he'd received from Colton.

Mark's arm burned with pain. The blood soaked through the bandage. Earlier, he'd used a spare shirt to wrap himself up, hiding the wound under his coat. He hadn't intended to get this close to his companions.

The last thing he wanted was to put them in jeopardy.

When he'd first seen them out the window, he'd been inspecting his wound with the flashlight, coming to grips with his fate. He hadn't meant to signal them. During the battle with his brother, he'd been bitten. Now, he was as condemned as Colton had been.

It was ironic. Mark had spent months denying what his brother told him, only to be cursed himself.

His plan had been to use the gun on himself.

At least that way, he'd be spared the agony of getting innocent blood on his hands.

He'd seen what the guilt had done to Colton.

And then he'd spotted the group out the window, seen the beast coming toward them. Tom, Ashley, and Billy had been attacked so close to the building that he knew he could make a difference. He'd decided to assist them and bring them inside. His hope was to share his story, to keep them safe, and to warn them.

When they were safe, he'd ask Tom to end his life. He'd have Tom bury him and Colton together.

But the urges were already kicking in, overriding his senses and his body. Each time he tried to speak, the beast inside quieted Mark's tongue, as if it were trying to preserve itself. The moon was like a silent foe.

And now more of the creatures — his brethren, as despicable as they were — were in the building. Even if Mark's fate were determined, he'd do his best to save his companions.

His head pounded from fighting the change. Sweat leaked from his brow. He recalled Colton's ramblings. According to his brother, some of the beasts were able to control themselves more than others. Colton had never succeeded in controlling his demons. He'd succumbed to depression and drink.

But maybe Mark could stave off his. Maybe he could keep his companions safe before it was too late.

His heart pounded so hard he thought it would burst from his body. His hands trembled on the rifle. A ripple of pain washed over him, pounding through his skull and extending down his arms and legs. His eyes felt like they were bulging from their sockets. It was only a matter of time until the change consumed him. Then he would be as powerless as Colton was, as condemned as the creatures downstairs.

The moon poured through the windows, spurring on his transformation.

He glanced over at Tom in the semi-darkness, but his companion wasn't looking.

Tom's focus was still on the door.

Chapter Thirteen

Ashley huddled in the storage room next to Billy, the smell of the dead body wafting into her nostrils. The room was a sickening mixture of grease, sawdust, and blood. She shined the flashlight around the storage room, taking in the shelving, the ceiling, and the floor.

The room was dank and uncomfortable. She'd rather be anywhere else than here.

But hiding out in the room, like most things in life, had become a game of patience. She glanced over at Billy, taking in his soft countenance in the glow of the flashlight, and smiled.

"How'd I do?" she asked.

"Great," he said, smiling back at her. "They have no idea."

He brushed his shaggy hair from his face. She leaned in close and nuzzled his neck. As disgusting as it was to be cooped in the room, surrounded by the blood of their brethren, it was only a matter of time until they succumbed to their true selves.

Once Tom and Mark were distracted, she and Billy would make their transformation. They'd spring from the closet and partake in what they'd been waiting for. In truth, Ashley had hoped for a larger crowd. But she'd settle for Mark and Tom.

Her main concern was that the others might reach them first.

She wanted them for herself.

"Should we go out there?" Ashley asked innocently, batting a playful eye at Billy.

"Give it a minute. Wait until they're good and distracted," Billy said.

She nodded. She trusted Billy. Billy was the most logical of the pair; Ashley tended to be impulsive. If it were up to her, she would've eviscerated Mark and Tom a while ago. In fact, she would've killed Tom in the street when they first met him.

Ashley and Billy had killed many times in the past, but always in secret, always in remote areas. They'd never bided their time like this. That was the promise they'd made each other when they encountered Tom—that they'd wait for a better opportunity, hoping he'd lead them to other survivors. Her goal had been to get inside the shelter before turning. That way they'd have a roomful of victims to themselves. But they couldn't wait anymore.

They were going to lose their prey if they didn't act.

Somewhere deep in the building, she heard the snarls of her brethren. Footsteps pounded the last set of stairs and feral cries filled the air. Ashley felt a sensation of warmth, of rightness, in what they were about to do. It was a feeling she'd had ever since the storm started. It was a feeling she could get used to.

They'd all known the storm was coming. It was as ingrained in the beasts as the need to kill. But none of them knew the exact timing. Until a few hours ago, it was nothing more than a feeling in her bones, an instinct as primal as the phases of the moon or the chill of winter. A few of their kind had even moved north in anticipation.

And now the storm was upon them.

She looked up at Billy, admiring how far they'd come. She was so glad they'd found each other. They'd learned to control their urges over the past few years together.

They'd started with Billy's parents.

Dave and Sherry were always trying to keep them apart, restricting their time together, limiting their interactions. And so she and Billy had lured them out into the woods a few summers ago. When they were far enough into the wilderness, Billy and Ashley had changed, killing them and disposing of their remains.

Ever since, she and Billy had been inseparable.

It was moments like that one that made her feel invincible.

Moments like that, and the one they were about to have.

"You ready?" she asked Billy.

"You bet." He smiled.

She sucked in a breath, recalling the guns Mark and Tom had. They'd have to surprise them. But that wouldn't be an issue. Not as long as she and Billy were together. They'd get through it, like they'd gotten through everything else.

She and Billy held hands as they started to change.

Chapter Fourteen

Tom listened to the clatter and chaos from the ground floor of the building. The creatures scraped at walls and overturned objects. Tom imagined them falling over each other like animals in a pet shop cage, fighting for scraps, the weakest among them destined to die. But he knew that was far from the case.

None of the things were weak, and if anyone was destined to die, it was he and his companions.

He gripped the gun with anxious hands. He felt like an inmate on death row, waiting for the final walk. Animal footsteps hit the stairs below. Nails clicked on the cement. He imagined the things loping on four legs, using all their limbs to make the climb. He recalled what Mark had said earlier. There were two other floors below them. Both locked. His last, frantic hope was that somehow the creatures would get hung up or distracted, that they'd never make it to where they were hiding.

He knew the chances of that were nonexistent.

The creatures had gotten into the building; it wouldn't take them long to knock down less fortified entrances. Besides, they probably smelled them.

Pounding ensued on one of the doors below them. Claws scratched wood. Creatures snarled in savage, intermittent bursts. The creatures were on the second floor landing. For a moment, Tom imagined that the beasts were on the hunt for someone else, and he was merely eavesdropping. It was hard to imagine he and his companions were the targets. He prayed the lower door would hold, if for no other reason than to buy him time.

The door burst open, crashing against the inner wall. The beasts tore through the room below them. More feet pounded on the bottom stairs, a swath of creatures joining the others. The noises were louder and more amplified than before. *They're right below us. Sniffing us out.*

Tom looked down, as if a set of claws might burst through the floorboards and pull him under. He looked over at Mark. Mark's body shook; he looked panicked and wild. After a few chaotic seconds, the noises changed direction, heading back for the stairs.

The creatures mounted the last flight.

Tom swiveled back to the door, staring at the machines and boxes in front of them as if to double the barricade's weight and size.

Inhuman feet scratched the staircase. And then the first, raging claw pounded against the wood fifteen feet away. The noise sent shards of fear through Tom's body. The pounding was so incessant, the growls so loud, that for a moment Tom thought the beasts were already inside the room with them. He recalled Billy and Ashley, hiding in the storage room. *Maybe they'll survive. Maybe they have a chance, at least.*

He pointed his weapon at the door, keeping a steady aim. His rifle felt small and insignificant. Wood splintered. One of the machines groaned.

Tom's finger shook on the trigger, begging him to fire, but he held onto his bullets as if he were holding onto his last breath of air. Once he started shooting, Tom knew he wouldn't be able to stop. The beasts would keep coming, and he'd fire until he was out of ammunition, out of breath, or both.

A loud crack split the air. It sounded like the creatures were already inside. It took a second for Tom to realize the noise wasn't coming from in front of him, but from behind.

He spun to find the storage room door open.

The flashlight—Ashley's flashlight—spun in circles on the floor, illuminating two shadows that were emerging from the darkness. In the intermittent light, he caught glimpses of the couple they'd left behind.

Only the couple wasn't the couple anymore. It was two of *them*.

Billy and Ashley were changing, their shapes twisting and transforming, flesh becoming fur. In a matter of seconds, their faces went from human to animal, noses elongating into snouts, teeth enlarging. Ashley—or the beast that had formerly been the girl—took a few staggering steps forward, closing the gap between them.

"Mark! Look out!" Tom shouted.

He spun and made a grab for his companion. Only Mark wasn't Mark anymore, either.

Mark had changed, too.

Chapter Fifteen

Tom dove for the far side of the room. His heart beat like a jackhammer. He got to his knees, took several frantic steps back, and fired his rifle. He wasn't even sure what he was aiming at anymore. The bullet struck the far side of the room, its path indiscernible. The creatures were coming too fast.

Holy shit, I can't believe Billy, Ashley, and Mark all turned…

I can't believe I'm alone…

But there was no time to process the surprise, only time to react. Tom ran further, searching desperately for cover. The room was bathed in an ethereal white glow. He located a machine and scrambled behind it, sticking his gun out the side. One of the creatures bashed against the other side. The machine inched backward, and Tom scrambled to move with it.

The beast hurled itself against the machine again, forcing it backward, sending Tom reeling into a pile of nails and tools. He couldn't see what he was stepping on, but he knew enough not to fall. One of the machine's wheels dug into his ankles, and a spark of pain shot up his leg. He cried out and fell backward, hitting the wall with a thud. The creature growled. It leapt on top of the machine. He saw its gaping maw in the glow of the moonlight. It swiped for his face; he ducked to avoid its claw.

A howl pierced the air.

Another beast collided with the one on top of the machine, taking it to the ground. Was it Mark? The two of them fell, tangled in a flurry of limbs. Tom couldn't even tell who was who anymore. He'd lost track. In just a minute, Tom had gone from a roomful of companions to a roomful of beasts, and for the second time that night, he was confused and alone.

The two beasts clawed and spat, fighting each other in a rage. They slammed into the machine again and rolled in another direction, sending tools and equipment tumbling to the floor. Were they fighting over *him*? Tom sank lower in his perch, trying to make himself invisible. His only hope was to ride out the nightmare.

His chances of survival were slim. Even if the beasts destroyed each other, there were still the creatures pounding on the door. Sooner or later, the room would be overrun.

The third creature flew past the other side of the machine. Tom thrust his gun over the top and fired again. The bullet glanced off something on the far side of the room. He had no idea what he'd hit. Between the shock and his nerves, his aim was awful. He waited for the thing to come after him.

Only it wasn't coming for him. It was racing toward the others.

Across the room, the fighting continued. The two beasts ripped at each other, punctuating the air with cries and growls. They slammed against the walls, shaking the room and adding to the compendium of noise.

The pounding on the door continued.

The gunshots might as well have been bait for the beasts on the other side, luring the remainder of the things in. It was only a matter of time until the door caved.

Tom regrouped behind the machine, clutching his weapon. The third beast had immersed itself in the ensuing battle. It sounded like all three were in a vicious tangle, intent on shredding each other to death. Tom wasn't certain what was going on, but whatever it was had bought him time.

He needed a course of action, a means to escape.

He couldn't battle all the beasts with the two shots in his gun.

He glanced around the room, taking in the silhouettes of the other machines, the windows on the far wall. Once again, he dismissed jumping. He peered around his hiding spot and caught a glimpse of the open storage room door, the flashlight still shining on the ground.

Maybe he could hide in there. It was a last, desperate attempt, but it was better than nothing.

Across the room, one of the beasts cried out in pain. Another howled. It sounded like one of them was wounded, perhaps in its death throes. The other two continued fighting, tumbling across the floor. Claws scraped against wood. Loud, throaty growls filled the air. Tom felt like he was in some devil's den, an arena encased with ice instead of fire. The winner of the battle didn't matter, because whoever was left would feast on Tom.

The machines against the door started to slide.

Tom peered out from his hiding place. The figures across the room were little more than a blur of movement. Tearing sounds emanating from in front of him—awful, horrific noises that reminded him of Desmond, of Lorena, of Abby. He stepped out of his hiding place, intent on running for the storage room.

And then the noise subsided.

Tom glared over the top of the machine. Two beasts turned to face him, eyes glowing. They were about fifty feet away. Tom raised his rifle at the larger silhouette, aiming for center mass. They stared at him, as if they knew what was coming.

Time slowed to a sludgy crawl.

Tom squeezed the trigger. The bullet struck the center of the thing, inciting a blood-curdling shriek. It threw its claws in the air, giving a last baleful shriek, and then collapsed to the floor. He aimed at the other. Fired.

But the second creature had already sprung. The bullet struck it in the stomach; it howled in pain, but it didn't stop. It shook its head from side to side, casting the pain aside.

Then it sprang for Tom.

Chapter Sixteen

The second beast was Ashley. Tom could tell by its smaller size, though its demeanor was no less frightening. The other two beasts were on the ground, their moonlit forms lifeless.

Tom squeezed the trigger again, hoping he had a bullet left. He didn't.

The creature — Ashley — staggered toward him.

Tom turned on his heel and raced across the room. Ashley followed, her feet scraping the wood floor. He'd wounded her, but at the moment, that didn't matter. She was still alive, and she was coming for him. He wove aimlessly through the room, narrowly avoiding tables and boxes, trying to get away. To his left, he heard the creak of weakening wood. The door shook with the fury of the beasts. He wasn't sure how long he'd avoid Ashley while they were locked in the same room. It was a battle of speed and energy.

The only thing keeping him alive was the beast's wounded condition.

He spotted the storage room door. It was still open. He saw the dim glow of the flashlight Ashley had dropped earlier, splashing over Colton's dead body.

He veered in that direction. It was hardly a

place of safety, but it was *something*. He skirted past a small table filled with objects, making a grab for something—anything—that might help him, but succeeded only in knocking several tools from their perch. Ashley was almost on him. He felt her hot breath on the back of his neck, her guttural cries laced with pain.

He'd almost reached the storage room when Ashley batted him from behind, knocking him off his feet. Tom flew through the air, landing on his gun, the wind knocked from his stomach. He rolled to the side, terrified of being filleted. But Ashley had already descended. The world became a suffocating mass of fur and blood. Tom kicked and squirmed, clutching the gun, his face buried in the creature's stomach. He pushed upward, trying to move, trying to *breathe*. The smell of musk and blood—of stretched, transformed skin—made him gag. The creature slammed him into the ground. Pain burst in his shoulders.

He shoved again, but the beast had a firm grip, its resolve deepened by its impending kill. He felt himself slipping into a world devoid of hope, absent of everyone he knew. The beast slammed him to the ground again. He saw the glint of its teeth as it opened its jaws.

Instead of being afraid, Tom was consumed with anger.

He thought of Lorena. Not the gutted, disemboweled carcass in the woods, but the smiling woman he'd lost. These creatures had taken her. They'd taken everything. He gave another thrust, using the last of his strength, and this time, the creature budged. Its claws ripped free from his coat. He gritted his teeth, smashing the empty rifle into its stomach.

He must've hit its wound.

Whatever he hit, he wasn't sure, but it was enough to send Ashley reeling off him, howling in pain. He rolled and moved in a half-crawl across the floor, contending with dust and debris, heading for the opposite end of the room.

His only thought was to gain distance from the beast.

The creature grabbed hold of him, tossing him into the side of a table. He pulled himself upright and resumed crawling.

He heard the barricaded door crack, and the noise in the hall grew louder. Several boxes tumbled from the top of the machine.

He wheezed for breath. The smell of the creature invaded his lungs, as if it was still on top of him, smothering him. The beast was right behind him. Tom stood and staggered. He heard the ragged breath of the wounded creature, its claws clicking the floor as it loped after him. He picked up the pace, stumbling across the room. A thought hit him.

A goal.

He followed the thin light of the windows, scanning by the room. His hip collided with the corner of a table. He cried out in pain and kept going. Ten feet from the door, he saw a pile of Mark's ripped garments. Ashley was almost on top of him. He glanced in all directions. Finally, he spotted Mark's gun. It had landed at the base of one of the windows. The beasts must've knocked it away during the scuffle.

Ashley leapt at him. Tom dove.

He heard Ashley hit the wall behind him, snarling and shrieking. He was almost at the weapon. Just a few more steps and he'd have it...

He claimed the man's gun and fumbled, trying to decipher which end was which. The light of the window behind him illuminated his hands, but in his panic, he wasn't sure of anything. His heart pounded uncontrollably.

He spun and aimed.

Ashley had recovered from hitting the wall. Her red eyes glowed in the dark. She let out a roar and pounced.

He fired.

The bullet hit its mark, striking her in the face, but Ashley kept coming, the gravity of her pounce setting her in motion. She slammed into Tom at full force, knocking them both over the windowsill and against the glass. The window shattered.

All at once, they were falling.

Tom kicked his legs to find footing, but found none. The gun flew from his grasp. Cold air and snow whipped at his face, stinging his cheeks. Pain lanced his side. The creature had a hold of him, clutching him in a firm, final death grip.

Even if he'd already killed it, it'd take him to the other side. He'd never survive the fall.

The ground sprang to meet them—a blurry mass of white.

Tom's last, panicked thought was to put the beast between him and the ground. He twisted and spun, clutching the thing's ratty fur, burying his face its stomach. And then he was hitting ground, the beast's body beneath him, sinking into the snow.

Both Tom and the creature's bodies shuddered from the impact. Tom heard the soft rain of shattered glass around him, and then everything went quiet and still.

Tom lay still for several seconds, listening to the whipping wind and the cries of the creatures inside the building. His pulse beat in his neck.

Am I alive?

He moved his arms and his legs, testing one limb at a time. Then he craned his head, inspecting the white world around him. He'd landed beneath the snowline. For a brief moment, he imagined he was buried beneath a drift, encased in a world of white. But the tips of trees and buildings in the distance proved otherwise.

Tom's body stung from the impact. His shoulders ached from where the creature had slammed him into the floor; his bare fingers were numb and caked with snow. His mouth was bitter with the taste of fur and fluids. He spat. The creature below him was still warm.

Warm, but limp.

The smell of its body sickened him, and he rolled to get away from it, suddenly feeling claustrophobic. But he couldn't. The creature had him in its claws. *Shit, shit, shit!* Tom kicked frantically before realizing its lifeless claw was still embedded in his coat. He pulled its arm free and fell flat on his back.

The wintry moon peered through the storm's glaze, mocking him.

His eyes roamed to the window. The height he'd fallen from was dizzying, even from the ground. He pulled himself to his knees, vying for footing. His head spun, and he held out his arms to steady himself.

He searched for the rifle.

He finally located it fifteen feet away, the barrel poking up from the ground.

He waded toward it, ignoring the burning pain in his body. Growls spit from the building, as if the structure itself might uproot and follow him. His only instinct was to retrieve the weapon and protect himself. He walked like a man possessed, his sights fixed on the handle. Snow cascaded in front of him, marring his vision, sticking to his face. His hands were cold and sticky with the creature's blood. When he reached the gun, he pulled it loose from the snow.

He spun. He aimed.

Movement flitted past the upper-floor windows. The things weren't outside. Not yet. He wasn't sure where they were, but he had no time to spare. He tore his eyes from the building and trudged in the opposite direction.

The snow tugged at his boots, like a white demon trying to pull him underground. He evaded its grasp and kept going. He eyed the rusted pickup truck. For a second, he considered running toward it, but Mark had the keys. Even if Tom could get inside, it would only provide temporary reprieve.

The SUV was equally useless.

His eyes darted to the building they'd been watching before — the one where the woman had been.

They'd gotten her, too. The door was closed; the windows were broken.

Shit, shit, shit...

He considered making his way over, hunkering inside the building, but he'd find little safety inside.

He gazed up the street at the station wagon. The vehicle was still; the headlights were smashed.

But Tom noticed something he hadn't before.

There was something trailing from the back of it. Thin plumes of exhaust were wafting into the air.

The vehicle was still running. The surprised occupants had never shut it off.

He huffed cold breaths as he veered from the

parking lot to the street. The air was freezing; any warmth from his body was counteracted by the wind. He'd lost his knit cap. His fingers were frozen on the handle of the rifle. With each step, he expected to hear the crunch of footsteps on the snow, pursuing him. But all he heard was frantic commotion inside the building.

Get to the car...

Tom felt like a piece of game roaming blindly into a predator's landscape, a mouse dropped into a snake's cage. Each step brought him closer to the maws of death.

Mark's words echoed through his head. *Driving is like sending a homing beacon to those things.* But they'd already been detected inside the building. They'd been detected at his house with Lorena. Was any place better than another?

The car was a gamble. But so was everything else at this point.

Another crash echoed behind him; the things were thumping down the stairs. In a matter of moments they'd exit the building. He was halfway to the car. *Maybe I should've headed for the building.*

It was probably too late, either way he sliced it.

Chapter Seventeen

Tom pushed himself as fast as he was able. He ignored the images that wracked his mind and the noises behind him. He convinced himself the station wagon was the physical incarnate of safety, wrapped in a two-ton casing of metal and wires. He clomped across the snow, his mind repeating the steps he'd need to take to flee the scene.

Get in the car. Close the door. Reverse.

The station wagon had come to rest against one of the buildings. His guess was that it was stuck in drive, motionless without a foot to press the pedal. As he got closer, he repressed the idea that the car would be wedged in place, that he'd be as powerless as the people who'd been pulled from the interior.

There was no time for doubt.

Somewhere behind him, the creatures crashed through one of the doors. The noise escalated from a contained din to a full-fledged roar. Footsteps and snarls escaped from the building's interior, filling the air.

Tom refused to look back. He forced himself onward, knowing a second's hesitation would cost him his life.

His boots slid on hidden ice. Tom grabbed

the air, nearly falling, but kept his balance. He kept going. The station wagon was thirty yards away. Twenty. He skirted around the half-buried remains of the vehicle's occupants, holding back vomit. He saw an arm. A torso. Body parts so mangled and caked with snow and blood that he could barely identify them.

Keep going!

He closed in on the vehicle, changing direction enough that he saw dots of movement in his peripheral vision. The beasts had surpassed the parking lot in half the time it'd taken him to traverse it. But it didn't matter.

He was at the car.

Tom banged into the rear bumper, following the outline of the vehicle until he'd reached the driver's side door. He flung it open. The window was smashed out, the interior riddled with glass. He heard the crunch of snow somewhere behind him. He leapt inside.

Revved the engine. Reversed.

The car whirred and groaned for several seconds before it started moving. His eyes instinctively flicked to the rearview. A mob of beasts canvassed the landscape, striding toward him. He cried out and hit the accelerator. The car flew backward, crunching over the tracks it'd made, spinning out in the snow. He changed gears and hit the gas.

All at once Tom was cruising forward, the station wagon gliding back and forth over the snow, the all-wheel-drive proving true to its namesake. A legion of creatures ran in pursuit, flooding the landscape, but he was several hundred yards ahead of them.

You pieces of shit. He rounded the corner and hit the gas, pushing the vehicle faster than was safe to drive. If he were to escape, he'd have to gain distance, no matter what the cost.

He'd rather die than let them have him.

He took another turn at the end of the block, the engine grinding, gaining more of a buffer zone. He kept his eye on the rearview mirror, watching the creatures disappear. He kept staring, even after they were gone.

The vehicle swerved and the tires spit snow. He flexed numb, stiff fingers. His body felt like it was coming apart at the seams — beaten and sore and exhausted. His mind was plagued with the things he'd seen, the people he'd lost. Lorena. Abby. His neighbors.

In spite of that, Tom felt more focused than he had in hours.

He clutched the steering wheel and took another turn, approaching West Main Street. His body was rigid in the driver's seat.

For the first time all night, Tom Sotheby knew exactly where he was going.

Outage 3: Vengeance coming soon!

ABOUT THE AUTHOR

T.W. Piperbrook was born and raised in Connecticut, where he can still be found today. He is the author of the **CONTAMINATION series,** the author of **OUTAGE,** and the co-author of **THE LAST SURVIVORS**. In addition to writing, the author has spent time as a full-time touring musician, traveling across the US, Canada, and Europe.

He now lives with his wife, a son, and the spirit of his Boston Terrier.

REVIEWS

If you enjoyed **OUTAGE 2: THE AWAKENING,** please take a moment to leave a review! Leaving a review ensures that the world will never have a rainy day again. OK, that's a lie. But I'd really appreciate it!

If you have a question or comment about **OUTAGE** or the **CONTAMINATION** series, you can connect with me at the places below. I'd love to hear from you!

Thanks so much for reading!

Want to know when **OUTAGE 3: VENGEANCE** will be out?

Email: twpiperbrook@gmail.com
Website: www.twpiperbrook.com
Facebook: www.facebook.com/TWPiperbrook
Blog: www.twpiperbrook.blogspot.com

Want to know when the next book is coming out? Sign up for **NEW RELEASE ALERTS** at:
http://eepurl.com/qy_SH

ALSO AVAILABLE BY T.W. PIPERBROOK:

CONTAMINATION ZOMBIE SERIES:

CONTAMINATION PREQUEL - FREE!
CONTAMINATION 1: THE ONSET
CONTAMINATION 2: CROSSROADS
CONTAMINATION 3: WASTELAND
CONTAMINATION 4: ESCAPE
CONTAMINATION 5: SURVIVAL
CONTAMINATION 6: SANCTUARY

POST-APOCALYPTIC:

THE LAST SURVIVORS
(co-written with Bobby Adair)

OUTAGE 2: THE AWAKENING
Copyright © 2014 by T. W. Piperbrook. All rights reserved.
First Print Edition: June 2015

Edited by Cathy Moeschet.
Proofread by Linda Tooch.
Cover by Keri Knutson.
Formatting: Streetlight Graphics

Special thanks to Casey Skelton and Andy Brown for your feedback and critique!

For more information on the author's work, visit: http://twpiperbrook.blogspot.com/

Dedicated to Jennifer, who helps me through my own storms.

No part of this book may be reproduced, scanned, or distributed in any printed or electronic form without permission. Please do not participate in or encourage piracy of copyrighted materials in violation of the author's rights. Thank you for respecting the hard work of this author.

This is a work of fiction. Names, characters, places, and incidents either are the product of the author's imagination or are used fictitiously, and any resemblance to locales, events, business establishments, or actual persons—living or dead—is entirely coincidental.

Printed in Great Britain
by Amazon.co.uk, Ltd.,
Marston Gate.